In the Time of Love

In the Time
of Love

Naguib Mahfouz

Translated by
Kay Heikkinen

The American University in Cairo Press
Cairo   New York

First published in 2010 by
The American University in Cairo Press
113 Sharia Kasr el Aini, Cairo, Egypt
420 Fifth Avenue, New York, NY 10018
www.aucpress.com

Dar el Kutub No. 2262/10
ISBN 978 977 416 386 9

Dar el Kutub Cataloging-in-Publication Data

Mahfouz, Naguib
        In the Time of Love / Naguib Mahfouz; translated by Kay
    Heikkinen.—Cairo: The American University in Cairo Press, 2010
        p.   cm.
        ISBN 978 977 416 386 9
        1. Arabic fiction   I. Heikkinen, Kay(trans.)   II. Title
        892.73

1 2 3 4 5 6 7 8   15 14 13 12 11 10

Designed by Sebastian Schönenstein
Printed in Egypt

1

The narrator says:

But who is the narrator? Shouldn't we give him a word of introduction?

He is not a specific person who can be identified historically, for he is neither man nor woman, without identity or name. Perhaps he is the essence of whispers or words spoken aloud, moved by the indomitable desire to immortalize certain memories, spurred by a passion for aphorisms and admonitions, fascinated by emotions of joy and sadness, by a secret tragic ache, by the sweetness of dreams we believe could be realized one day. In reality he is a heritage woven of angelic history, its truth springing from its intensity and deep desires, embodied by a sure imagination which rushes to invade the heavens even though his feet trip on familiar earth, on cracked ground and crevasses spilling stagnant water. If I record it as it came down to me, recording it in the name of the narrator and in his very words, I am only complying with the commands of loyalty, carrying out the orders of love, while at the same time yielding to a force one cannot risk ignoring.

The narrator says:

In our neighborhood there lived a widow named Sitt Ain. A strong woman, wonderfully eccentric, provocative; a unique individual who could not be replicated, inviting caution in the presence of inscrutable life, which is limitless in its possibilities.

Her story usually begins when she was a widow of fifty with an only son named Ezzat, who was six years old. Why doesn't her story begin before that? Why doesn't it begin when she was a little girl, or when she was a bride? Why don't they talk about Amm Abdel Baqi, her husband? Why did she have no child other than Ezzat? And why did she have him at such an advanced age—was the fault hers or her husband's? But what does all that matter? The narrator is committed to his vision, and if he freed himself from it he would have to give up and investigate until he reached the realm of our father Adam and mother Eve. Therefore let the beginning be when Sitt Ain was fifty and her only son Ezzat was six, when she was a prominent woman, her prestige growing and expanding with time like a rising city. She owned all the large apartment buildings in the neighborhood, for she was very wealthy, in fact unexampled in her wealth. I don't know if she was the origin of the wealth or if it was her husband, but it can be said that her sister Amouna had nothing. True, that does not prove that her wealth was inherited from her husband, for it is conceivable that the two sisters once shared equally in a limited estate, and that Amouna squandered hers while Ain invested her part. In any case she was the richest person in the neighborhood, not excepting the master craftsmen and the merchants.

In addition to great wealth she was distinguished by excellent health. They say she still had the luster of youth at fifty years of age, without a single black hair having faded and without any complaint in any part of her body. She was firmly built, of medium height, neither weighted down by obesity nor marred by leanness. Her breasts were rounded and high, showing no traces of nursing; they were a concealed center of attraction at the front of her body, like transmission towers (in today's language), but wrapped in the restraint of dignity. Her best feature was her black eyes, radiating a peaceful light that melted in compassion. As for her nose, it was delicate but long, its length suitable for a man's face, like her wide, full mouth. People will tell you a lot about the pure wheaten color of her complexion, untouched by cosmetics, and about her white head-covering, her flowing gallabiya, and her dark cloak, for she was not seen in the street stuffed into a tight wrap or buttoned garment or concealed by a black or white face veil. She challenged wagging tongues with the dignity of her age, the gravity of her character, the charm of her conduct, and her impregnable position, proud of a reputation as fragrant as a rose.

In our neighborhood no one averts his eyes from any short-coming, and no shortcoming is safe from being discussed, remembered, and recorded. Nothing stays in the memory longer than the deeds of the fitiwwat, pimps, or prostitutes, to the point that we use them to date events, so the memory is associated with the life of Dabash, Danaf, or Aliya Kofta. For the story of Sitt Ain to pass without a single word against her is conclusive evidence of her purity, chastity, and abundant virtue. When she went out in the street she walked with an umbrella which never left her side, winter or summer; she protected herself with it from sun or rain, or she used it—in rare cases—to warn anyone she encountered who was drunk or high on drugs, and woe betide the dervish who so forgot himself as to meddle with her. The truth is that she was protected not only by her chastity, but above all by her strong personality.

By virtue of her financial interests she met with many residents and business associates, and they would quickly recover from the spell of her beauty under the influence of her strong voice, her serious logic, and her piercing gaze. Not even fitiwwat would allow themselves to be lulled into carelessness in her presence, and they might leave a meeting with her muttering, "What a man!" But that meant no more than frustrating a cunning fox or defeating a swindler. Her manliness was only a style she found appropriate for business dealings in a neighborhood whose ways she knew better than anyone. It was neither flawed femininity nor a coarse nature nor a mask to cover some defect. Certainly not. . . . She was rather the essence of mercy. She became a legend only because of her mercy. If she had kept to her house, the needy would have gone to her—and her house was the most beautiful in the neighborhood. From the outside it appeared only as an unpromising, dark stone wall with a thick gate frowning in the middle, bearing a stuffed crocodile at its summit and at the midpoint a dusty brass knocker, shaped like a man's fist. When the gate opened the house appeared, lofty and amply proportioned, betraying power and comfort. Extending behind it was a garden which exhaled an odor composed of the scents of jasmine, henna, and fruit, surrounding a fountain whose marble wall had been extended by wood ever since Ezzat had learned how to walk, run, and get into mischief. After she was widowed she no longer waited for the needy in her house but went out into the neighborhood with her umbrella, descending on them in their houses. She grew accustomed to a circuit of mercy, becoming a constant visitor in the tenements of the poor, plunging into the families of toiling women, of widows, and of the crippled.

The narrator says:

In her day the neighborhood forgot wretchedness, hunger, and nakedness and had no difficulty with what was needful for weddings or illnesses or burials. All cares disappeared together under the umbrella of Ain, Ain the compassionate, her heart beating with love, her generosity giving without counting. She administered apartment buildings for the sake of the humble. She was the soft rain flowing over barren land, leaving it green and ripe, dancing with the water of life. The mother of the neighborhood, who departed accompanied by pious prayers, by radiant smiles, and by abundant gratitude. They swore by her name, and retold her feats of generosity, the true, the miraculous, and the legendary. She would befriend, confide, and become intimately familiar with them before presenting the remedy, stealing into the depths of the wounded hearts, living with pain, associating with sadness, and becoming fond of the wretched, as if she were dealing with sons or fulfilling a mission confided to her by the forces of the unseen. It is said that she practiced charity in the life of her husband, Amm Abdel Baqi, in the confines of the house and to a limited extent, and then blossomed after she was widowed.

It was supposed that she would economize after being widowed, and that she would economize more out of love for little Ezzat, but she transcended the logic of things on wings borrowed from Paradise, despite her strong and deep mother-liness, for no woman was ever gladdened as she was by the motherhood that was given to her at an unexpected, critical time. She considered Ezzat heaven's gift to her lonely heart. She was captivated by gratitude to God the most merciful, and sponsored evening devotions for al-Hussein, al-Sayyida, and the saint Abul Su'ud, the healer of wounds. How many ages she spent gazing with an enchanted eye at the little face! Then she would move on to the path of charity, spreading the sail of mercy. Her long nose appeared in his face, and her pure complexion, and the protruding eyes of his father. She said, "He's a boy, not a girl, and what matters is the heart, so let the heart be sweet and compassionate." He was active and selfish, not relinquishing her without a fight. He was also destructive, trampling flowers, chasing ants, and killing frogs, and he would not go to sleep unless she was telling stories beside him. "Does he think he is a sultan?" she asked, laughing, with a thankful

5

heart and a spirit overflowing with contentment and delight like an unfolding flower. It occurred to her by way of playfulness to make him a caftan, robe, and turban; she stared at him merrily when he put them on, and then said, "How nice it would be for us to give them to Sheikh al-Azizi after you tire of them." Then she showed him to her friends who came seeking mercy, asking, "What do you think of this sheikh?" They answered, "A beauty, by the lord of al-Hussein, may God extend his life forever." She thought a bit about "forever," for she was as intelligent as she was devout. A spring cloud overshadowed her serenity, and she mumbled, "May my day come before his, oh Lord, and when the divine decree comes may his hands bury me." Quickly she remembered a past generation of loved ones, images of graves and tombstones invaded her mind, of cactus and sweet-smelling basil, pictures of people clothed in life, and she mumbled again, "They are alive with us, and none but God knows the unseen."

One day Umm Sayyida asked her, "How did you become the most noble of God's creatures?"

She humbly asked God's forgiveness, hiding her pleasure, which appeared in a quick smile like a flash of light in a cloud passing over the moon, and mumbled, "It is only God's mercy to a sincere servant."

Then she asked herself, "How can I know what it is that makes giving my pleasure in love?"

It was widely reported that when Ezzat came down with the measles she stayed up three days without a wink of sleep.

Time came and went. Our neighborhood changed visibly and brought forth new generations with dazzling qualities, and with some strangeness as well. They took a particular position regarding what was told about Sitt Ain, a position characterized by indifference, at times somewhat harsh.

"Why should we be asked to believe unquestioningly what they say?"

"It's a pretty story, but would it stand up to a thorough examination?"

"Don't you see that doubts hover even over scholarly history?"

"Charity is a real phenomenon, but not in this fashion."

"Don't forget that charity itself is one of the games of egotism."

"Here you have the fact of Sitt Ain, which love has erased: she was mad with mercy and charity, but she did not meet the eye that could plumb the depth of appearances, and if she had it would have revealed another woman, with a real human life, perhaps full of scandals."

Whatever can I say to answer that? I say what I said before, that our neighborhood always steps up to magnify and relate any flaws, but it does not recognize the good except when there is no escaping it. Moreover, Ain's story is not lacking in human weakness, a fact which confirms its truth and plausibility; but we refuse to concede to ideals because of long immersion in foul water. Courts are crammed with brothers, and anyone who falls by the wayside dies alone. I tenaciously believe Ain's story, for there is no story which does not express some truth, just as there is no pain which does not signal some wound. The truth of which there is no doubt is that Sitt Ain walks in her dark cloak and flowing gallabiya, with her ancient umbrella. A smile beams from her dignified face, gladdened by greetings, prayers for her, and admiring glances. She passes on her way to the shabby tenements, sits among the wretched, and calls out, "How are you, dear friends?"

She asks about Zaynab and Amm Hussein and Umm Bikhatirha, then she leaves the place, having showered them with mercy. How many are those who call for studying her in the light of the id, the ego, and the superego, and how many are those who hover over your sexual life, Ain! How many are those who delve deep into memories to unearth some scandal of yours!

The narrator also says: Ain adored the four seasons. We are accustomed to most people preferring a specific season or two seasons, but she adored all four seasons. She loved the winter, clouds and rain; its wind did not keep her from her rounds, intoxicated by sympathy, and its rain did not scare her off when it poured down on her unfolded umbrella and muddy water ran beneath her feet. She loved the summer, adjusting quickly to its heat, commending its sweet nights; and she adored fall, saying that it was the season of fresh washed beauty, its nights beguiled by confidences and good wishes exchanged on parting. As for spring, it was the season of the garden and of voices, the khamasin winds laden with messages from unknown distant lands, where hearts burned with sacred fire. Without a doubt, she responded to the changing seasons with her tolerant temperament and her deep-rooted faith.

Our neighborhood surges with feelings, emotions, and clashing voices, swept with storms, quarrels, and contradictory views. She would follow it all with calm and compassion, praying that the good would win out, no suspicion ever entering her heart. Her serenity did not come from indifference, for she probably knew—she was never cut off from people—where the good was and where evil lurked. As we said she prayed that the good would win, but she did not forget that all of the combatants, or many of them, were in need of her aid!

It is remarkable that in general those who do not think much of her did not live when she was active, did not live during the last period of her life, and did not witness its end. It is also remarkable that most of them emerged, grew up, and made

8

their way by virtue of her charity and mercy, but they do not know that or affect to forget it or interpret it badly, as we have seen. As the years blend into each other her life expands in the consciousness of the narrator, finally becoming a towering mountain; but like any other mountain it is exposed to the erosion of the elements.

2

One day—as the narrator says—Sitt Ain was seated under the arbor of jasmine, tossing bits of bread dipped in broth to a group of cats numbering no fewer than five, and Ezzat was standing between the arbor and the fountain in his striped gallabiya and sandals, grabbing with his small hand at the rays of the setting sun receding from the trunk of the lemon tree. Summer was in the last days of its journey, and only a little time remained before the cannon shot signaling iftar. Ain was feeding the cats by hand, united with them in mealtimes and in hours of companionship: the mother, Baraka, the color of tahini with a white star in the middle of her head; the father, Abul Leil, coal black; Anaam and Sabah from their progeny; and Nargis the gift of an outside family, all of them Persian cats with fluffy hair. The intimate relationship between her and the cats, the mutual understanding and exchange of ideas, the affection and harmony, the compliance and coddling, the closeness and secrets, all gave rise to stories and tales.

In the calm a voice was raised seeking permission to enter, "Hello in there!"

It came from the corridor leading to the entrance of the house. Ain smiled sociably and called, "Come in, Umm Sayyida."

The woman approached in her wrap, her face unveiled like all the toiling women of the neighborhood, followed by her little Sayyida, her hair combed and wearing green clogs. The two women shook hands while Sayyida spontaneously went to Ezzat, to watch his struggle with the rays of the setting sun. Although they were the same age (six), she was nevertheless four years older in experience and awareness. He glanced at her briefly and then returned to the rays; she stood watching him, smiling and silent. Ain said to Umm Sayyida, "I haven't seen you for three days, you false friend."

Umm Sayyida laughed from her thick throat and said, "Earning a living makes demands, dear lady."

Then, as she sat on the grass near Ain's feet, "Lord knows that if a day passes and I don't see you, it's not part of life."

The cats moved nervously between absorbed attention to the bread and staring at Ain with translucent, apprehensive eyes. Ain said, "You always find the right word. Are you busy with a new bride?"

"The matchmaker sees astonishing things. Who would believe that a groom would be refused for a copper pot?"

"What do you mean?"

Umm Sayyida saw that she had understood her intention, so she smiled and said, "He's a deserving young man!"

Baraka arched her back and raised her tail like a fountain, apparently sated. She jumped and landed on the bench next to Ain, who stroked her with the palm of her hand, Baraka responding like a dancing wave. Umm Sayyida wondered hesitantly, directing her words to the cat, "How are you, Nargis?"

Ain cried, "She's Baraka! See how you've forgotten the household?"

Umm Sayyida laughed, then spied Ezzat and cried, "How are you, Si Ezzat?"

He took no notice of her and Ain said, excusing him, "He's busy with the rays of the sun!"

Umm Sayyida laughed again and said enthusiastically, "The whole neighborhood smells of mouloukhiya."

"Is that what brought you, you glutton?"

The woman began to praise the aroma of jasmine and henna, speaking in the lengthened, melodious tones of flirting.

After the call to prayer Ain broke her fast with some lukewarm fruit compote then got up to pray the sunset prayer, while Umm Sayyida sat at the table, having removed its covering, and muttered, "There is no shame in hunger." A serving girl went to light the large kerosene lantern hanging from the ceiling over the dining table, then lit the lamp on the veranda overlooking the garden. The iftar meal passed, their eating punctuated by a few passing words. Afterward the two moved to the balcony, Ain sitting on the sofa, while Umm Sayyida preferred to sit on a cushion in order to stretch out her legs and ease her overstuffed stomach. She rolled a cigarette and it affected her from the first puff, her amber eyes drowsy and her thick nose inflated, smooth at the tip like a cat's head. Silence reigned for a while, under the urgent desire for rest. A serving girl brought Ezzat's colored Ramadan lamp, and Ain had a yearning to set out. She said, "How lovely it would be to take a walk in al-Hussein!"

Umm Sayyida muttered laughingly, "Once I can walk again."

She rolled another cigarette. Ain mumbled, "Thanks be to God, the night is beautiful."

Umm Sayyida shot her a long look and then said, "I have something more beautiful."

"You only have talk of marriage, or gossip about one of God's servants."

"It is talk of marriage!"

11

"Really? Do you have a bride for Ezzat?"

The woman said imploringly, "Rather I have a groom, or more if you like."

Ain looked at her suspiciously in the blue light of the lamp, and Umm Sayyida said, "And you are the desired bride!"

Ain waved her hands in protest and cried, "Damn you."

She said with mounting enthusiasm, "There is no real man in the neighborhood."

But Ain cut her off, "Have some decency, woman!"

"Dearest lady, you are still a beautiful young woman."

She said sharply, "If I wanted to get married I wouldn't have remained a widow this long."

"Why do you remain a widow?"

"Hush."

She scolded her, looking toward the old wall over which the full moon had risen, rich and deeply red, its light feeble as it began its journey. Umm Sayyida let her enjoy the view, but she insisted on returning to the subject, saying, "By the lord of the moon. . . ."

But Ain cut her off, speaking decisively, "Stop, Umm Sayyida, it's Ezzat and Ezzat only."

Then she realized she had been distracted, and wondered, "Where is the boy?"

Umm Sayyida disliked cutting off the conversation and said, "Inside, of course."

"And where is your daughter Sayyida?"

"She must be playing with him. He didn't go out; here's his Ramadan lamp waiting for him."

Ain rose. She descended the stairs of the veranda, plunged into the darkness of the garden until she disappeared completely. She reappeared after a while, dragging Ezzat behind her by one hand and Sayyida by the other, her voice wondering angrily, "Aren't you two afraid of hell?"

Sayyida ran to her mother and Ezzat stood hanging his head. Ain addressed Umm Sayyida, "It's that old curse, did you see?"

Umm Sayyida hid a smile, but she cried, poking her daughter, "God forbid."

"The boy is innocent, but your daughter. . . ."

Umm Sayyida muttered, "God alone knows."

"Keep your eyes open, Umm Sayyida."

"My eyes are always open."

She didn't forget to say to Ain, as she took her leave, "We will return to our subject."

But Ain said resolutely, "Close that door with lock and key!"

3

Uneasy thoughts circled in the familiar serenity. They weren't serious, but they troubled someone accustomed to tranquility. What was the real reason she was disturbed by the child's fooling around? The time had come for him to go to the kuttab, and there were men who were greedy for her money. She looked at the mirror in its ivory frame embellished by Quran verses and shook her head, remembering her promise the day his father died, that she would not allow a stranger to take the place of a father. Five years had passed and her resolution had not weakened. Only the seasons changed, the years passed.

What really occupied her mind was her sister Amouna. She was ten years older, so she was both Amouna's sister and her mother. She remembered their mother, most especially her death. Her grief at the separation was alarming, as her grief for her father had been, just as the separation from her husband set her heart aflame. Her grief was deep like her joy, but grief lived longer. No sooner would she visit the tomb than she would be moved and abandon herself to long confidences. They are alive like us, but only God knows the unseen. What really pained her was her sense that Amouna secretly envied her. For her part she did not begrudge her anything, but that does not uproot envy.

Amouna always said to her, "You are scattering what you have recklessly."

Ain would say, irritated, "The money belongs to God."

Amouna would answer, the beauty of her face disfigured by resentment, "As far as I know the money belongs to you, sister," and she would reply, mockingly, "In reality we own no more than two handfuls of dust."

"Why do you love to talk about death?"

"Perhaps because it accompanies our every step. Do you lack for anything?"

"You are all goodness and blessings, but I am grieved by the waste of money."

Ain looked toward a small carpet hanging on the wall, its design depicting the dome of the Aqsa Mosque, and cried, "God be my witness. . . ."

Then she stared at Amouna, saying, "Is money wasted when it comforts the distressed, feeds the hungry, supports the disabled, and cheers the child?"

"Show me any wealthy man or woman. . . ."

But she cut her off, "Enough. What you say ruins my peace of mind."

But she would always return to that talk like a donkey returning to his pen without being led. Therefore she did not doubt that the birth of Ezzat was a rock over which waves of greed broke. His birth altered the balance, changed calculations.

Umm Sayyida brought the Sudanese incense prescribed for such situations, saying, "Relatives! They are like scorpions."

Ain was pleased by the act of her lifelong friend, and asked her, "Do you know the secret of happiness in this world?"

"God make you happy always and forever."

"It is when we take only enough money to sustain life."

The narrator also says: On Lailat al-qadr during Ramadan, Amouna visited her, dragging by the hand her little Ihsan, who was four years old. As they sat on the veranda after iftar, Ain said to her, imploring, "Avoid what distresses me."

They sipped their coffee in peace, until Amouna said sweetly, "I want to try my luck on Lailat al-qadr!"

She prayed for her, saying, "May God give you good luck."

Amouna began to look at the cats as they settled in the corners of the veranda, and mumbled laughingly, "It's a house of cats."

"When they are full they pour out praise to God."

"You know their language better." Then she wondered, a little embarrassed, "Shall I try my luck?"

Ain said innocently, "You have to look at the sky the whole time."

"But my luck is in your hands, sister."

"Really!"

She said, as if it were a gamble, "Sister . . . what do you think about Ezzat and Ihsan?"

For some unknown reason Ain felt a foreboding, but she said, "Ezzat is my little son and Ihsan is your little daughter."

"Don't you understand what I mean?"

"It would be better for you to say it clearly."

"It's as obvious as Lailat al-qadr."

Ain cautioned seriously, "Do you have any knowledge of what will happen tomorrow?"

"That's why what we are able to do today is very important to me."

"Today, really?"

"Yes . . . let's write their marriage contract!"

"What a strange idea!"

"We are free to do as we please!"

Ain hated the idea and found it repugnant. She saw in it greed which must be eliminated. She believed her sister was in urgent need of a bath with a concentrated antiseptic. She cried, "I don't see any good in that at all."

"Ihsan is your niece."

"Amouna . . . it would please me for him to choose her himself one day."

"She's beautiful, as you see."

"I will not agree to the marriage of a child who has not yet entered the kuttab."

"They do that in the country, and that's the cradle of the sages."

"Only crazy people do that!"

Baraka suddenly darted off toward the garden as if she had smelled prey, and silence reigned, ominous and anxious. Amouna's voice erupted, altered, "Is that your last word to me?"

Ain said dryly, "Most certainly."

"You . . . you are cruel!"

"I ask God to bring you healing."

She said sharply, "I am not ill, Ain!"

"God only knows."

Amouna mused bitterly, "I wonder which of us is ill?"

"Your tongue is running away with you, Amouna."

She got up forcefully, saying, "You have hated me all your life."

"Really?"

"And you envy me!"

"I envy you?"

"Despite all your money you envy me!"

Ain said, averting her face, "Do not invite the devil into my heart."

Amouna shouted, "He already lives there!"

She broke out in sobs, taking Ihsan on her shoulder and moving to leave the place without farewell. Ain's anger turned into sadness. She said apprehensively, "Next time I'll find you in a better mood."

Amouna's voice came to her, "You will never see me as long as I live."

4

The kuttab of Sheikh al-Azizi opened its doors as the winds of autumn crept from their damp cradle. Ain resolved to send her only son to the sheikh.

"You will find honor and the light of God in the kuttab."

Honor because the sheikh was among the constant recipients of her generosity, and the light of God because it broke forth first and foremost from the Book.

But Ezzat asked apprehensively, "Isn't the garden better?"

She stroked his head with her palm and said, "It is part of becoming a man."

Ezzat remembered the groups of boys and girls as they left the kuttab in the afternoons. Their faces expressed no happiness with what they were coming from, no satisfaction with the deformed, dwarf sheikh. He shot her a baffled look, and she said, "Upright boys love the kuttab. In the kuttab we learn, and a man is respected only for learning. You must respect the sheikh as you would your mother. Don't let yourself be tempted to laugh at him, for that is forbidden and God will not pardon his servant for it!"

He remembered Sheikh al-Azizi, for his strange form was known to all: a dwarf with bowed legs, a protruding chest, and small features like a child, rocking from side to side as he walked, leaning on a short staff two feet or less in length, as if he were a toy like the ones displayed at fairs. Never would he forget seeing him one rainy day, when a well-wisher had placed him on his shoulder to take him across the street.

"I charge you especially to respect the sheikh."

She repeated that in a clear voice and he felt foreboding over separation, and apprehension before an unknown experience.

She continued, sharpening the look in her beautiful eyes, "And with the girls behave in a way that pleases God!"

He dimly imagined the thicket under the cover of night and blushed, moving his head in embarrassment. She mumbled kindly, "As for the past, God has accepted your repentance."

When Sheikh al-Azizi received the news in the parlor—sitting on the edge of his seat with his feet dangling two handspans above the floor—his face beamed, and he said, "How long have I waited for this day, so that I might return a thousandth part of your favor."

But when Ezzat sat crosslegged in the first row on the mat in front of the sheikh's seat, he seemed like another person. He neither welcomed him nor encouraged him with a smile; it was as if he had never seen him nor heard of him. He also marveled at the icy gaze fixed in his eyes and the sternness that clothed his small face, while the boys and girls sat in silence, enveloped in awe and ruled by an unknown force. Where was the toy that eyes would follow, with sympathy and mockery, in the street? Now he was a sultan in his kingdom, exercising unlimited power, the stripped palm branch at his side threatening rebellious hands and feet. Ezzat was certain that he was a captive, defenseless and without distinction, the same applying to him as to the others; he resolved inwardly that he would not attend another time.

He noticed Sayyida at the end of the row and their eyes met for a moment in what seemed like a smile, then she quickly ignored him. He was annoyed by the air of equality reigning over the session, all alike on a single mat and he without the distinctions he enjoyed in any other place as the son of Sitt Ain and the young lord of the great house. It was an unbearable new situation; perhaps his mother knew nothing about it. Next to Sayyida he saw a girl of similar age whom he had not seen before. He found her very attractive. She had a round face and glowing complexion with two lively black eyes. She made a strong impression on him, delighting him, easing his pain, and making him forget his sadness. He wondered what part of the neighborhood she lived in, this sparrow who had been forcibly removed from her nest. She was the girl carried off by the ghoul whom the sultan rushed off to rescue. How sweet her voice, as she repeated after the thin voice of the sheikh, "Praise belongs to God, the lord of all being." At any rate the kuttab wasn't all bad, and Sheikh al-Azizi would not harm him.

When lunch time came he sat facing the wall like the others. He untied the knot of his napkin, spread it out, and had begun tearing his bread into pieces when he heard on his right, "What have you got?"

Ezzat saw a boy of his own age, his eyes narrow but pleasant, with a strong jaw and a flat nose, who seemed simple and lively. He disliked his intrusion, but he could not avoid answering, "White cheese and halvah."

"Great, I have falafel and tahini salad. Let's eat together."

He did not wait for his acceptance but spread out his napkin until the edges met Ezzat's napkin. He pointed invitingly at the falafel as his hand reached for the cheese, then he introduced himself, "Hamdoun Agrama."

The other was forced to say, "Ezzat Abdel Baqi."

"I know . . . Sitt Ain's son!"

He disliked having his name mixed with cheese, falafel, and tahini salad, but he did not find Hamdoun annoying, and he liked the cleanliness of his gallabiya and cap. Hamdoun said to him, "You're not hungry?"

"I get full quickly."

Hamdoun was not satisfied with the answer, but he happily devoured the food.

They left school together. Hamdoun didn't leave him, and soon Ezzat began to like him. Hamdoun said to him, "We'll play together and study together and eat together . . . okay?"

He inclined his head in agreement, and the other said, "And a devil might jump out at us from the tunnel, so it's best if we're together."

"I don't go near the tunnel at night, and my mother has memorized the Quran."

All of a sudden Hamdoun called, "Badriya!" Ezzat followed his eyes to the 'sparrow.' The girl looked at them with a smile and then took off running.

He asked him, "Do you know her?"

"Our neighbor . . . Badriya al-Manawishi."

He liked being friends with him better.

Ain met him with a look that was searching and sympathetic, and mumbled, "May the journey to manhood be blessed for you."

He said listlessly, "What a boring place!"

"You must love it, it will make you a respected man."

He grumbled, "I sat on the mat like the others."

"We are all children of Adam and Eve, and the best is the one who works the hardest. That's why I put food like everyone else's in your napkin; your food is waiting for you now. Don't avoid anyone."

Going along with her, he said, "I met a lot of them."

"Really? Tell me some of them."

"Hamdoun Agrama."

"Ah . . . an orphan who lives with his mother's sister. She's a virtuous, kind woman. Who else?"

He was silent, at a loss. Then he said, "Only him!"

"A lot, but they produced only one! How many girls are there?"

"Four."

"New to you?"

"All except one."

"Sayyida?"

"Yes . . . and I learned the name of another when someone called her. Badriya al-Manawishi."

"Ah—the daughter of Umm Ramadan. She might be the last of the children from the most recent husband. Her mother has been married five times or more."

He looked at her with interest. "She has five husbands at one time?"

She laughed and said, "You will learn that a woman has only one husband, but she can marry another if she is divorced."

He asked her with increasing interest, "Will you also marry another?"

"Certainly not."

"Why?"

"Because I don't want to. Now come on and eat a bite, it will make you strong."

A little before evening a servant came and announced the arrival of a boy called Hamdoun Agrama.

5

His life in the kuttab was not easy, for he was often reprimanded, but he was never flogged. Sheikh al-Azizi knew that he could not go beyond certain bounds with him. Ezzat advanced over a bridge filled with stumbling blocks. Hamdoun's abundant energy sometimes helped him, or at times kindled his enthusiasm. Their friendship had become real. Over time he met all the boys, but Hamdoun remained his one friend. Ain welcomed him, pleased by his neat appearance and precocious desire to study; she hoped Ezzat would find in him encouragement to work. She said that he was a smart boy who loved to study without anyone pushing him to it. She hoped for a bright future for him to compensate him for being an orphan. She said to him more than once, "May God open a way for you. If you keep up your hard work you won't leave school to learn a handicraft."

She began to invite him to lunch every Friday. Because of that she invited his aunt Sitt Roumana to visit her, and a good relationship was established between them. Sitt Roumana's husband was a merchant in large tents and their furnishings, renting them for weddings and funerals. He made a good profit but he had ten children. In spite of that, Sitt Roumana was fond of Hamdoun and treated him like any of her children. He had inherited a small piece of land from his father, which could be sold if need be and its price put to use. Sitt Roumana acknowledged more than once, "I love him for his hard work. You won't often find someone who works so hard at his age."

Thus the friendship was auspicious for both sides, bringing them ample, innocent happiness. Like all boyhood friendships it wasn't without idle disputes, such as the defeat of one of them at hopscotch or four-in-a-row, and Sitt Ain's son was not one to accept defeat gracefully. But the differences never went beyond an hour's rift, and soon a concession would come from Hamdoun!

Playing in the lane was an entertainment Ezzat couldn't escape, which then became something he sought happily when Sayyida and Badriya joined them. No one disapproved, as long as the playing took place in full view and in daylight. Badriya monopolized the two boys' attention to the point that Sayyida felt she was an extra and nothing more. Her cheerfulness did not help her; her luck was hidden in her dark complexion and rounded nose, a repetition of her mother's nose. Ezzat was dazzled by Badriya's face despite his young age, and his heart was ahead of his years in being affected by a vague emotion, distilling desires from a fantasy land with no existence outside of the imagination. In order to monopolize her attention he told her about his house and its furnishings, and about the garden and its fruits and flowers.

Sayyida said, "I know all that."

Ezzat said, "But she doesn't know."

Badriya said, "We only play in the lane."

Hamdoun said, "Sayyida comes to the house with her mother."

Ezzat said to Badriya, "Your mother should come to visit us, and you with her."

Badriya said, "My father doesn't permit my mother to go out."

Sayyida tried to attract him as much as she could but he paid no attention to her. The memory of the thicket might come to his mind, but it was coupled with pain, fear, and shame. As for Badriya, he looked at her with a marvelous imagination, happy and lively, promising the joys of this world and the next.

He spent two years in the kuttab, blessed with a happiness known in this world only to those who weave together innocence and imagination.

The moist winds of autumn stirred from their cradle as they had in years past, but this time they announced a new separation, sharp and painful: they warned that the intoxicated boy was about to be evicted from his paradise. He was presented with a new decision, directing him to the elementary school to take the entrance examination, and this time the presence of Hamdoun alongside him was no inducement. Badriya and Sayyida had left school and were forbidden to play in the lane; Ezzat's ardor flickered and his spirit languished. Hamdoun passed the entrance examination while Ezzat failed in arithmetic, although a fortunate visit to the school changed the result and enrolled him, unwilling and unhappy. Sayyida was not cut off from his domain as she continued to visit the house, usually in the company of her mother. He became more and more accustomed to her appearance, her dark complexion becoming familiar, the roundness of her nose normal, her liveliness endearing and her conversation not lacking entertainment. As for Badriya he only saw her very rarely, usually in the company of her father. He would steal a quick glance from her, and she would pass by in greater seriousness than was likely at her age, as if she had not shared his life's joys with him for two years. He had enough opportunities for work and play to distract him from her, but he was not able to free himself from her memory, or to erase from his memory his singular fondness for the glow of her face.

He seemed to have trouble with his studies, days passing without a single mark of approval, and he did not become accustomed to school. He longed for freedom and for the garden. One day he heard another pupil say, pointing to him, "Why does he need to learn when he's the richest person in the neighborhood?"

He was amazed at his mother's insistence on tormenting him. He was little affected by Hamdoun's excelling. Hamdoun would encourage him to work, and if it were not for his persistence in studying with him Ezzat would not have made any measurable progress. Hamdoun would say to him, "Your mind is excellent but you're lazy."

Ezzat would wonder scornfully, "Is it important for me to work hard?"

Ain said, following the conversation with interest, "Of course, how lovely are the successful! Knowledge is part of faith and you are among the true faithful."

Yes. He loved devotions and was infatuated with stories, but he was prematurely sad.

His mother continued, smiling, "You need to study more and to eat more."

Hamdoun agreed, "He is really thin! At school they say that his mother spends her money on the poor, and that the son can't find anything to eat!"

Ain laughed and admonished, "Learning and food."

Hamdoun said, "He's preoccupied with heaven and hell!"

Ezzat said to himself, with heaven and hell and Badriya. Then there was his mother, who was the fabric of his life, his dreams, his joys, and his fears! She was the connection between him and God, the connection between him and life, she was everything, and that's how they looked at her in the neighborhood. From his earliest consciousness he had been accustomed to her comings and goings, to her tours crowned with glory and love under her umbrella, to her meetings with poor women in the garden. He learned to consider that a kind of marvelous worship, and in the light of the comments that reached his ears about her active, abundant generosity, both in school and elsewhere, he began to look at her with new eyes, and to unconsciously compare her with other women. Surely she was not the only wealthy woman who did that . . . until he heard Hamdoun say once, and he believed him, "She's the mother of the neighborhood, not just your mother."

But the amazing thing was that this rare power was of no use to him in intimate matters, for no help could be expected from her for his complicated lessons, and no relief would come at her hands to return him to the lost paradise of Badriya. His mother cared for wounded hearts and left him to suffer alone, leaving him as the years passed and the gloom did not lift.

One day Hamdoun came to him, his eyes sparkling and moving lightly. For some unknown reason his heart shuddered with a clear, sad memory of Badriya al-Manawishi. They sat on the veranda as the sky emitted a drizzle that washed the leaves and chased away the sparrows. Hamdoun began to say, with marvelous enthusiasm, "A world! A world like no other."

He stared questioningly at Hamdoun, who said, "Yesterday my uncle took me and some of my cousins to the Egyptian Club."

"The coffee house!"

"No, the theater. We saw a play from beginning to end."

He described the details of the trip to him in great precision—entering, sitting down, the hall, the curtains, the actors and actresses, the story, the singing, everything. "There you laugh, you're transported, and sometimes you cry."

Ezzat couldn't imagine anything much. The picture of Paradise was clearer in his imagination, and likewise the picture of hellfire. Hamdoun said, "You'll see it one day. . . . But we can copy it right here, on this veranda!"

"How?"

"I'll teach you what to say."

Without hesitation he began to adapt the play, creating the scenery by suggestion, then he said, "Now you are a girl called Juliet and I am a boy whose name is Romeo!"

Ezzat frowned and asked, "And why shouldn't it be the other way?"

Hamdoun said compliantly, to avoid arousing his anger and stubbornness, "Fine."

The short dialogue went as Hamdoun imagined it, and he acted what he could of it, but he did not succeed in convincing Ezzat to act. Ezzat imagined Badriya in the role of Juliet. This was the story, but where was the girl who had the real role?

Ain followed the scene from the window of her room. She didn't understand anything, and said to herself that children come into the world bearing marvels. She recited the Throne Verse from the Quran, her heart overflowing with sympathy for the orphan.

Hamdoun changed perceptibly. His fascination with the theater never wavered. He filled some of his free time with a new hobby, reading; with some difficulty he would read whatever publication he could get his hands on, advertisements, magazines, detective novels, finding his way at last to *A Thousand and One Nights*. Through him, Ezzat became fond of detective novels; he never read anything out of love except for the Quran and detective novels.

Hamdoun said, "It will be a great summer vacation, we'll act out every story we read."

Ezzat said, "Let's take the stage to the lane."

"That's an idea. Is your mother bothered by the game?"

"Not at all, but we might bring in some actresses."

Hamdoun laughed and began to smooth his prominent eyebrows, saying, "An impossible idea."

"Isn't Badriya your neighbor!"

"But between us there is a wall stronger than the wall of the ancient tunnel."

But he saw her, perhaps every day, and that was worthy of envy.

At the end of the fourth year they each passed the examination for the elementary school certificate. For Ezzat passing was a miracle. Sweets were presented to them in the garden.

Hamdoun, aged twelve, announced his desire to become an actor and a playwright. Ezzat smiled and did not believe him. Ain said, "Choose some work, not playing."

His zeal was stronger than they imagined. Ain asked her only son, "And you?"

He shrugged his shoulders in indifference. He loved two contradictory things, religious devotion and dominion. He was proud of his mother and his house, and his heart loved rank. He was not haughty but he secretly hoped to be his mother's successor, perhaps in the house and the neighborhood, or in the house alone! Ain murmured, "I would like to see you great."

He did not know precisely what greatness was but he hungered for it in his heart.

6

High school was a new era.

Windows opened to a current of new information, then warm air poured forth, opening the innermost chambers and ripening the deepest folds. A new person grew from the depths of Ezzat . . . and Hamdoun as well. The tip of his nose changed shape, his voice deepened, and he was agitated by obscure desires. Ain prayed for the soul of Amm Abdel Baqi, and said that Ezzat was just like him even though he hadn't known him. She said that from now on breezes would blow laden with fragrances and anxieties. In that period, Hamdoun became a devoted reader, varying his readings and digging for every word related to the theater. Ezzat was immersed, in his free time, in reading the Quran and detective novels.

He would almost have forgotten Badriya, were it not for a passing encounter that assaulted him forcefully once again. At sunset he was walking in the lane toward Hamdoun's house, and Badriya was crossing the lane to the house opposite. Encouraged by the short distance and her father's absence she had come out in her dress with her face unveiled, the image of a ripe female with her face even more glowing and pure, her svelte stature, and two braids hanging all the way down her back. They were at almost the same point under the shadow of the sunset and exchanged looks, smiling with shared memories and filled with affection. Quickly he whispered, "Hello."

She whispered shyly, "Hello."

She hastened her steps, tripping, fragrant with her first youth. He stood below Sitt Roumana's house as the sunset enveloped him profoundly, slowly turning him into a ghost. He needed to stand still to regain consciousness and balance, to renew his connection to his surroundings. He realized with emotion that he was fated to love Badriya forever. Love looked to him like life itself in its attraction and arbitrariness. His deep sense of dominion left him and he felt that he was alone. He did not want to remain long in Hamdoun's house as it was crowded with his family, so they quickly left together. They headed for the Egyptian Club and on the way Ezzat said, to ease his mind, "I saw Badriya on my way to you."

Hamdoun murmured, "I see her often."

Ezzat surrendered to an urge and said, "I love her."

Hamdoun said, laughing, "Same here."

Ezzat asked him uneasily, "You love her too?"

"Did you expect me to hate her?"

"Of course not. . . . But I mean something different by love."

The other said calmly, "Not in that way."

"Tell me the truth!"

"When have you known me to lie?"

He relaxed somewhat but his heart knew no certainty. He had never wanted anything and refrained from it except for the world of girls. But yesterday was not today. He shaved morning after morning, perhaps to speed the appearance of his whiskers; but he did not know how to send the message of his love in his neighborhood, with its ancient iron bars. If he raised his head a hundred other heads raised with it, questioning and suspicious, and he still trailed the garment of shyness and piety woven by his mother's pure, long fingers. A lapse was excusable but it didn't pass without a harsh accounting, and where could he escape the watchful eye of God?

He began to go to the theater regularly, at the constant urging of Hamdoun; and Hamdoun began to dream of writing and secretly tried it, allowing only Ezzat to read it. How he would have liked to change the course of his life, but he continued his education with the goal of finding a stable job. Ezzat continued his education out of pride, and in order to please his mother.

The mother was not unmindful of what was fermenting inside him. She was worried that he might slip and disobey God (exalted be his name), and she refused to flee from her responsibility, or to leave him alone to confront the devil. She took courage from the darkness of the garden when they were sitting together one evening in spring, and said to him, "The time has come for me to treat you as a man."

He laughed shortly. For her part she thought about her sister Amouna. She was anxious to make peace with her. She had sent Umm Sayyida to her; she had visited her herself.

She had brought her to visit her as before, but Amouna remained reserved. Ain resolved to make peace with her in a practical way. She said, "Ezzat . . . one of the basic rules of godliness is that we protect ourselves by marrying."

The word "marrying" lit up the bower and Badriya appeared, illuminated.

Ezzat mumbled in astonishment, "Marrying!"

"Yes, you are a man!"

"I haven't yet gotten my high school baccalaureate."

"People marry without getting degrees."

Ezzat asked, laughing, "Are you going to Umm Sayyida for help?"

"But we have a bride, your cousin Ihsan."

Ihsan was beautiful, inclined more than she should be to plumpness, a warning that she would take after his aunt Amouna. He felt no real attraction toward her. He said clearly, "No."

She asked in displeasure, "Why, sir? The girl is perfect."

"Perhaps, but there's nothing I can do about it."

She asked sadly, "Won't you help me make peace with my sister?"

"Not in this way."

"Do you dislike the idea of marrying now?"

He said frankly, "The truth is that I don't dislike it."

She asked with interest, "Do you have your eye on another bride?"

"Yes."

She said with concern, "Things are happening behind my back. Why didn't you tell me from the first day? Who is it?"

"Badriya al-Manawishi."

She was taken aback for a few moments as the silence spread; then she said, in a tone of regret, "No."

"No? Don't you like her?"

"Her mother marries a lot."

"I'm talking about the girl, not her mother."

"A girl takes after her mother!"

"That's an unreasonable judgment."

"There's no disagreement about it."

"I don't believe that!"

"Your mother is never wrong."

He said with some sharpness, "Let me try my luck."

She implored, "Don't disrespect your mother's opinion."

He said in annoyance, "I also cannot disrespect my own wishes."

"I very much want you to marry but I'm intent on your happiness."

He said forcefully, "I will only marry according to my own purely personal wishes."

She sighed and said, "This is a new tone, Ezzat. Naturally you are free, but I am not pleased."

He was dispirited. He did not take angering her lightly; could he take a step that would displease her? He said, "If it weren't for you I would not have thought about marrying now at all."

She did not speak. Her silence weighed heavily on him; he began to suffer inwardly. He said decisively, "Let's forget the words we've said."

He lingered alone in the garden after she left, feeling as if she were still there in her place. He felt himself carried away by a harsh anger toward her, more like hatred. It was a passing hatred, however, quickly giving way to the shackles and humility of love. But he could see her with a critical eye, as if he borrowed

32

it from the chirping of the crickets. If she wished she could turn into a solid rock, all springs of mercy dried up in her heart. This amazing woman who fraternized with the poor, made friends with cats, and made an enemy of her own son. How often she had frightened him with devils, and here the most revolting devil was embodied in her obstinacy.

Ain sighed in profound sadness, saying that the boy was stubborn. Stubborn like his father, and like his mother also. She made up her mind not to give up on him when he was the jewel of her life. He was also foolish like his father. If Amm Abdel Baqi had not bent to her will in the end he would have been lost like a speck of dust. Yes he loved the girl, and the girl was truly beautiful, but what good was love that strayed? Marriage set love free, and then he would find before him nothing but a woman dreaming of another man. Just so, her mother lived moving from one man to another. I am responsible for him today; tomorrow he will be independent and commit his own follies.

She summoned Umm Sayyida and asked her dryly, "What do you know about Ezzat and Badriya?"

The woman was shocked and asked in turn, "What about Ezzat and Badriya?"

She cried in warning, "Don't deceive me!"

"God forbid!"

"So what do you know?"

"May God forgive me."

"Not a heart beats in our neighborhood without your taking its pulse."

She said heatedly, "I don't care about rumors."

"I care about them."

Umm Sayyida exhaled and said in a low voice, "They talk about love. As you know, they make mountains out of molehills."

"They are talking about his love for her?"

"Yes."

"What do they say about her?"

"Nothing, you know her father."

"How do they back up what they say?"

"Worthless things with no basis, a passing glance for example."

She said in distress, "That can lead to scandals. Tell me the truth, Umm Sayyida, have they met even once?"

"God forgive me. The girl lives under the power of a stern father."

"You know the mother?"

"Sure."

"What do you think of her?"

"Nothing good."

"Has she learned of what's being said about my son?"

"It's not unlikely."

"And the father?"

"Impossible."

"Has Badriya's mother talked to you about this?"

"Certainly not, but she did ask me to look for a suitable groom, and hinted at Si Ezzat and my close relationship with his mother. But I knew your opinion of her, so I made the excuse that Si Ezzat was still below the age of marriage. I suggested Hamada Effendi."

"What did she think?"

"She wasn't thrilled."

"Naturally, as long as she's dreaming of the stars." She shot her a harsh look, making Umm Sayyida avert her eyes in shame. "And you hid all this from me."

Umm Sayyida said heatedly, "I didn't want to bother you with talk coming from Badriya's mother."

Ain leaned toward her, frowning, and said, "But you will not hide from me a single thing related to this topic?"

34

She said, breathing easily for the first time, "You have my word on that, as God is my witness."

When Umm Sayyida left Ain she poured out her worry to Baraka, petting her and murmuring, "I'm suffering, Baraka. Pray for me for peace."

7

The love went on growing and swelling like a date palm. He relieved his cares with the theater, but immersed himself in detective novels in his free time. When Hamdoun appeared with his strong features beaming, he would feel an obscure foreboding, envying him his progress and dedication to his goal. Ezzat often retold the story of his love, and Hamdoun would sympathize with his distress with the warmth of a loving friend. He said to him once, "It seems to me that your mother doesn't think much of love."

Ezzat said, "She doesn't think much of the girl's mother, and that's unjust."

"Love is also suspect in our neighborhood."

"Crime novels are more beautiful than reality!"

"Yes, more beautiful than the reality of our country."

He went on to talk about tyranny. He was concerned about that, his concern increasing as he got older, and his talk didn't lack bloody expressions. Unlike his friend, these matters didn't seriously move Ezzat's heart, but he said, "It is within our power to resist tyranny, but how can we cope with a mother like mine?"

Hamdoun said, "Still, no one can deny that your cousin is beautiful!"

He was irritated, and his obscure fears stirred once again.

They received the secondary school baccalaureate the same year. Ain congratulated him, her face filled with joy, but he said to her, "No—love is over between us!"

She did not take what he said seriously, and replied jestingly, "Do you know the number of girls dreaming of marrying you?"

"But I want only one."

"You only want her because I don't want her."

"Rather it's as if you are refusing her only because I want her."

"Would you like me to tell you the stories about her mother?"

"Her mother does not concern me in the least."

"But she's lurking deep within her."

"Let's suppose the marriage fails—am I incapable of divorce?"

"And the failure...? Do you think it's without consequences?"

During the summer, Ezzat chose to enter law school. For his part Hamdoun decided to get a job, both to relieve his aunt and to give the rest of his day to the theater. During that time it became known that Abdel Hamid al-Koumi had asked for Badriya's hand and that the Fatiha had been read. The news ripped out a heart—perhaps more than one—by its roots and the garden looked yellow in Ezzat's eyes, exhaling a poisonous odor. Had he been relying on the hidden magic of love alone? Had he imagined that it—the magic of love—could keep his beloved until he was able to emerge from his passivity? He cried to his mother, confident of her unlimited power, "Do something."

She asked in alarm, "Do you want to snatch a girl from her man?"

"You are the one who made it possible for him to carry her off!"

She stammered in compassion, "God's choice is blessed."

36

He shot her a look that grieved her and went out. He found Hamdoun seething with emotion. Ezzat said, "I'm burning up when I should have set the fire."

Hamdoun asked, "Is it over?"

Ezzat took Hamdoun with him to Badriya's father, and asked him to keep Badriya for him until he became independent. The father said, "We have read the Fatiha. Your mother could have spoken had she so wished."

Hamdoun said, "He is the one who wishes."

The man said, "I am an upright man and I do not deal with deception."

Ezzat knew loneliness while immersed in a crowd. He grieved as a strong man does when he is defeated. He realized that his rank was counterfeit and that its light was derived from his mother. In reality he was poor, miserable, and powerless. Anger blinded him to the point that he lost his senses. A power erupted from him that smashed his mother's head, an evil power striding in the cloak of an angel. He killed her seven times, each time with a special weapon; other times she died naturally. If he were as strong as Hamdoun he would set out on solitary adventures, welcoming the life of a vagabond. But he was the captive of the garden, of soft cushions and of that obscure, unknown force. Because he was so attached to life he had lost life's splendor. He was faithful to his fetters, singing the anthems of suffering. Badriya would move out of the range of his hope after making an indelible imprint on him; and he was fated to wait for a hope that would not return, to seek a being that did not exist. A curse on pride that was taught to the gullible in the cradle of captivity.

In the thick of the futile struggle he received a letter from Hamdoun. Hadn't he met him yesterday and every day?

Dear Ezzat,

You must understand in the name of lifelong friendship. It is a true friendship, firm and pure. You must not think ill of me. I had reconciled myself to sacrifice, on the condition that you do something. But you declared your powerlessness and accepted reality. At that point I decided that I had the right to act. Like you I am in love but I will not let her go with al-Koumi. We are going to run away together to get married far from the family and the neighborhood. I have a little money from the price of the land, and I will depend on that until I find a job. I will not give her up, just as I won't give up the theater. Your friendship and its beautiful memories will remain with me. Do not think ill of me,

> Yours sincerely,
> H. Agrama

He read it many times before he comprehended what it meant, and he killed Hamdoun many times—more than his mother—before he understood his position. How skillfully he had hidden his love from him. Truly he was an artful actor. He did not forgive him even though he had not suspected him. Maybe he was mocking him. Maybe it would have been better for al-Koumi to take her. He was used to his wishes being carried out before he made them known, and what had happened behind his back? The world was teeming with criminals like Ain and Hamdoun and Badriya. Killing served no purpose. Worse than that was eyes filling with tears, the yellow of the garden deepening, the sparrows dying. To have come to be without a beloved and without a friend and without a mother.

The story of the elopement spread through the neighborhood like dust on a stormy day. The storm scorched him as the defeated hero of the story. It burned Badriya's father and mother and Sitt Roumana, Hamdoun's aunt. Animosities erupted. Rumors of the event recorded a perfect tale of scandal: Badriya's mother was divorced following a violent quarrel.

He was sitting in the arbor one searingly hot evening when he saw his mother's shadow spread on the ground in front of him between the fir and the stream. She approached, saying, "We haven't exchanged a word in days. It's hell."

He looked at her sagging, subdued face, where a lifeless look had replaced joyful radiance. He showed no sympathy for her and averted his eyes. She said softly as she sat down, "You should know me better."

He avenged himself by drawing out the silence. She said, "The time has come for me to admit some things to you." In the silence rose the croaking of the frogs and the chirping of the sparrows. She continued, "I made it my business to know everything and I thought about yielding to your wishes, and then I got some unexpected information."

He listened closely but did not speak.

"There was mutual love between her and Hamdoun. That was God's decree and no one is to blame."

He cried unconsciously, "He was betraying me!"

"Never, he's a loyal young man. He wasn't in an easy position; I don't know what was going through his mind but in any case he did not wrong you." She sighed deeply, and continued, "I was forced to insist on my refusal. I saw no use in revealing the truth." She brought her sad face close to his, kissing his forehead, and said, "Don't give in to grief. Life is stronger than anything. Consolation will come to you more quickly than you think, and you will find someone better."

At that point Umm Sayyida came, preceded by her crude "ahems." He left the place in the deepening twilight, and in the hall he met Sayyida coming to join her mother. They shook hands. Suddenly he was ablaze, with no preparation or preliminaries, for no apparent reason. He was gripped by what swept over him. He did not release her hand. He went inside, pulling her by the hand. She submitted without any real opposition, taking courage from the dark. He did not utter a word, embracing her. She was stunned and dumbstruck. He obeyed an indomitable, obscure fate without the least thought for its consequences, as if he were playing alone in the dark with no partner. Base submission, hidden desire, and the thrall of memory overspread the utter loneliness, and indelible inscriptions were carved on the black tablet of the night. . . .

8

Love was no longer the sole occupant of the place; now it was rivaled by a new fate: fear. Sometimes he became oblivious to love, staring at the new apparition. It was a stable apparition, neither wavering nor weakening with the passage of time. It was the one mistake that never tired of pursuing him and demanding a solution. Sayyida in herself was nothing, but because of the mistake she had become everything. Now she was hidden in a corner of existence, tiny and unseen, plunged in weakness, but her voice hummed like a cricket. Her father had died long before, her older brother was in prison and the younger had emigrated. Her mother was dependent on his mother's charity, but the mistake had demolished one structure and raised another in its place.

What could he do? The depths of his mind were unaccustomed to suggesting solutions, but they were tireless in killing. The look Sayyida had given him during a passing encounter was fixed in his imagination, full of shared signs, docile, timorous, despairing, assuring him that what happened could not pass as if it had not happened. She was his hidden sadness when it took human form; sometimes a hidden sign escaped her, recounting a complete tragedy, a passionate, silent appeal begging for charity or mercy, like the last shudder of a frog before giving up the ghost. What could he do? Unwillingly he remembered Hamdoun. Why? Perhaps because of his insistent prattle about the weak and the strong, because of his views with which he wanted to reform the universe.

He was reading a chapter of a detective novel when he thought he heard his mother's voice blazing in the garden. He looked from his window and saw the two women—his mother and Umm Sayyida—deeply immersed in some conversation. He was overcome with a gloom like the lingering twilight. Something would happen, someday. He expected it the way someone with a toothache expects his molar's throbbing pain.

He heard his mother's footsteps coming; he cursed his fears and shot from fear to defiance. She sat pale-faced on a sofa in the middle of the room. She fluttered an ivory fan with a nervous motion of her hand, and the strange thought crossed his mind that the miracle that was his mother would be destroyed by his hands.

Ain said, her voice shaking, "What does this house lack?" She hesitated a bit and then answered herself, "The Quran is recited in it, it is fragrant with incense, and it is girded by fair dealings and good intentions, so how could the devil sneak inside?"

Ah . . . it had happened . . . and he had to pretend to keep reading.

41

Ain asked in sorrow, "Have you not yet felt my presence?"

He asked stupidly, "What?"

"Can't you guess what's behind my sadness?"

He closed his book and looked in surrender at the flourishes in the Persian carpet.

"What's this that Umm Sayyida has revealed to me?"

His face went pale and he did not speak. She sighed, saying, "Why should I torture you? It's senseless to scold when it's too late."

He saw with clarity—perhaps for the first time—a silver censer set on two brass legs below the purple curtain.

"Listen my son, you aren't the first person the devil has deceived. What's really important is how we deal with the mistakes we make." She sighed audibly and said, "We are rich, but that's worth nothing. A man's worth is defined by his relationship to his Lord, although we are called to account according to our capacity."

He found himself slipping down a single path with no outlet.

Ain continued, "We may err but we cannot be unjust. We must make restitution for our mistakes, and the more the restitution goes against our own desires the closer we come to pardon from our Lord." She raised her head as if she were intent on the lamp and said resolutely, "You will marry Sayyida at the first opportunity." Then she got up and said, "It is a decision that brooks no discussion; what attests to your good nature is that you welcome it."

Events followed in quick succession, as if they were happening to another person. The news spread through the neighborhood and created general astonishment, just as it struck like a lightning bolt in the houses of the brides who had been proposed, because of their beauty and family, for such a unique groom. How could Sitt Ain refuse Badriya al-Manawishi only to take Sayyida, the daughter of Umm Sayyida the matchmaker? Was the secret to be found in some skill of Umm Sayyida? Was the explanation in some deviant taste that came over Ezzat? As usual the bad interpretation hastened to hiss its suspicions, and it hit on the truth this time by pure chance.

Thus Ezzat was married at eighteen years of age in a union contrary to his tastes and inclinations. Thus Sayyida moved into the most beautiful house in the neighborhood to occupy the highest place in it. Thus Umm Sayyida became the mother-in-law of the most prominent man. Amouna raged in rancor and cut off her relationship with her sister forever. Ezzat surrendered to the fait accompli as he would to an inescapable fate. True, he did not consider the verdict final, only a necessary temporary solution until he could rid himself of it at the appropriate time. His grief for his lost love redoubled, and he considered the entire ordeal a just recompense for his weakness and hesitation. From the first moment Sayyida realized that she was not favored with her husband's love, or even with his pleasure. The life she tasted was cold, purely animalistic, without any tenderness or respect. Moved purely by an instinct for self-preservation, she hid under Ain's wing, giving her perfect loyalty and fidelity from a wounded, deprived heart. Her mother counseled patience and unfailing courtesy. She said to her, "You have a Lord, so depend on him only."

The young woman said to her, "I would rather go home."

The woman insisted, "Don't renounce your blessings. Know that men don't stay in any one state, and married life is nothing but a battle."

In that atmosphere devoid of sweetness, Sayyida became pregnant and bore Samir. She became a mother, Ezzat became a father, and Ain became a grandmother; so even in the worst of circumstances she was able to change the dimensions of her small universe, to release in it springs of new, unknown emotions. Ezzat's heart was moved. A new love came to rival the old love, whose pain was so familiar that he had become accustomed to it. As for Ain, she was crazy over the newborn and loved him passionately, and Sayyida's heart aspired to a better life.

Ezzat was not successful in his legal studies, finding himself without ambition or ardor, so he left the school two years after entering it. He was uneasy in a life with neither love nor friendship, so he decided to find a job. He wanted to achieve a measure of independence, to fill the void and to experience the life of a government employee, fascinating for so many.

He took a job in the ministry of education. It didn't take long for him to develop an aversion to the position and its hostile atmosphere. His mother advised him to invite the employees in his office to a banquet in the house, to strengthen his position and to defend against the stratagems of the sly. He had spent a month at this work when his mother asked him, on his return, "Haven't you set a date for the banquet?"

He answered calmly, "There was a quarrel between me and my superior."

She stared at him with concern, and he said, "I tendered my resignation," then burst out laughing.

9

The narrator says:

Years passed, one after the other. His old love was submerged in a sheath of tranquillity and languor. His relationship with Sayyida was still composed of cold feelings and rough deeds. No kind word slipped out, and he did not hesitate to insult her for the slightest lapse, and sometimes for no reason. He would take Samir far from her to enjoy complete freedom in playing with him and kissing him. He was ill at ease in his life after the disappearance of Badriya and Hamdoun, and detective novels did not fill the void; he fell into a hashish den to forget his troubles, and there learned where to spend his night until daybreak, and how to flee into sleep until midday. Ain watched his new life with concern, and would say to him, "We make our happiness with our own hands."

He resented her for her perpetual happiness. She went about like a bee collecting the nectar of charity and love. She was well into her seventh decade with complete immunity from the symptoms of age, making her rounds ceaselessly, blessed with energy, nimbleness, and radiant joy. It was as if she meant to make him suffer when she said, "Son, treat your wife kindly, for she is a rare woman in her patience and propriety."

It vexed him that she had proved the innocence of her stand with respect to Badriya, and he was eager to condemn her. He held against her the obstinate position she took about his love before she knew about the love between Badriya and Hamdoun. In any case she was guilty. He was torn between loving her and hating her, and sometimes he dreamed of her death. But how could this skilled woman die? He would precede her to the grave. He would live in thrall to her his whole life. She derived an extraordinary power from the unknown. Could he bear life without the inward knowledge that she was to be found somewhere in the house or the neighborhood?

She would repeat her urging that he treat Sayyida well, and he would wonder what had made him keep her throughout the years that passed.

The fact was that he didn't love her and didn't want her. Because of Samir? Or was it his eternal weakness that kept him from acting? He said to Ain, in answer to her entreaties, "The time has come for me to divorce her."

She spread her hands to heaven, stammering under her breath, "God save him from the cruelty of an animal."

"I don't love her."

"Kindness is needed more when one does not love."

"The problem is that you are happy, but as for me, I'm a miserable man."

She clasped his hand tightly and implored him, "Don't think about divorce, even if you decide to marry another."

What was the sense of bringing in another woman without love?

Ain was a happy woman, and the happy don't see the truth.

She was scattering her wealth and life was passing. He said to her, "You spend without counting."

"Thanks be to God."

"But it's also my money!"

"To my knowledge it is God's money, be He praised and exalted."

He asked, laughing, "Haven't you heard of sons killing their mothers?"

She answered him, also laughing, "But I know that you love me, that you will fill my grave with your tears, and that my body will float on them."

Sayyida seized an opportune moment of calm free of bickering and said to him, "What you really need is work."

He asked, mockingly, "Shall I work as a matchmaker?"

She ignored his innuendo and said, "Create some suitable work; your mother won't begrudge you the capital."

The idea took hold of him. He disliked its coming from Sayyida but it invaded him. He mumbled, mockingly, "Strange that a good idea should come from you."

She said, sighing, "Try it, and God be with you."

He did need work and independence, but where would he get the experience? Where was that damned Hamdoun? He hadn't mastered anything in his life other than reading crime novels—and smoking drugs in the hashish den. Here was another dream dawning in his arid life.

10

No action followed Sayyida's suggestion. He dreamed of the project and became more weary with life. He found nothing new in life except for one new habit, which was eating a great deal under the influence of the drugs to relieve his boredom. He lost his youthful slenderness and began to put on weight.

In that period he forgot his old love, or nearly so, and became characterized by an enveloping apathy; even his devotions became practices without feeling or ardor. He found only Sayyida before him, and made her responsible for his deterioration. The young woman suddenly rebelled against her position and rushed to Ain, who was wrapped in her abaya behind the window, watching from behind the glass as the rain poured over the garden, washing the leaves and filling the streams. She vented her complaint to her and said, sobbing, "I must return to my mother."

Ain did not remove her eyes from the water and the trees, absorbing her rebellion in complete calm. Then she asked, "Do you have any mother but me?"

She stammered in grief, "You are everyone's mother, but I am suffering."

Ain asked, turning toward her in compassion, "Are you still ignorant about men?" Then, pinching her cheek in affection, "They need constant education, extending from the cradle to the grave, and that is our task."

The other started to speak, but she silenced her with a sign and continued, "The woman who abandons her house is ignorant and does not deserve the blessing of motherhood. What has changed you, after I believed that you were the most intelligent of all women?"

"How long should I put up with being insulted?"

"He insults me with his actions more than he insults you with his words, so should I abandon him in turn?"

"But. . . ."

She cut her off, "Be careful not to cause trouble for the little prince."

He would steal glances at the young women who once had dreamed of marrying him. They came and went in the neighborhood, sheltered by marriage and rectitude. Any one of them was more beautiful than Sayyida. Any one of them was fit to create a love, if it was not abundant at the beginning. He lived intimately with them in his imagination, his inhibitions weakening with the weakening of his devotions. Among them, Itidal was known for a certain spiritedness, so he was emboldened once to address a whispered greeting to her, which was met with a harsh frown. The mistake had consequences, for he was surprised by Sheikh Salam al-Darwi, headmaster of the primary school, who pounced on him in the hashish den, and in full view of the company spat in his face and yelled at him, "You despicable coward!"

The scandal spread and its details became known. Some people made the excuse that it was only an innocent greeting that escaped him innocently and inadvertently, while the majority disapproved of it without denying his good intentions. The sheikh and the younger man scuffled together until the others separated them, and Ezzat went home with a swollen lip.

For the first time blame was directed against something pertaining to Sitt Ain. Sayyida hid from others' eyes to cry alone. As for Ain, she stood before Ezzat in a military posture and said, "Tell me the truth, has the devil deceived you?"

He said with false intensity, "Certainly not. I swear that to you."

She said, sighing with satisfaction, "I believe you. But you erred."

She invited Sheikh al-Darwi, honored him in every way, and assured him of the innocence of her son. She kept him with her until lunch and made peace between him and Ezzat, her mind not resting until she was confident that the dark cloud had completely dissipated.

But it did not dissipate in Ezzat's sky, he alone knowing of his lie, his hypocrisy, and his cowardice. He felt that his devotions had lost their spirit and serenity, and that all that remained of them was a hidden compunction exhaling grief. He yielded more to the temptations of rich food and began to dream about the proposed project. He also dreamed of abandoning the neighborhood, which no longer held any promise.

Ain learned from him of his desire to start a commercial enterprise and welcomed the idea. She said, "I have thought about that for a long time, but I waited for the thought to come from you!"

He was not pleased by her welcome and felt an obscure fear. But Ain continued, saying, "You don't have any experience, but that's no reason to give up. The people around us work in wood, flour, coffee, and canvas. Let me place you as a partner with one of them until you learn the trade secrets, then after that you can continue with him or be independent with similar work in another place."

He found himself on the threshold of a decisive change that would turn his way of life head over heels, and he shied away from it. Would he free himself from the current order easily? He spent the night in the hashish den, slept until midday, and entertained himself with crime novels; would he give up all of that all at once? He said, "Great . . . that will happen, without doubt . . . but let's wait a while to carry it out. . . ."

His desire to abandon the neighborhood became more urgent, and he began to voice his desire in Sayyida's hearing. The young woman was distressed; she knew full well that her married life owed its survival up to now to Ain. In his caution not to anger his mother he did not cross the line in abusing her, but what fate would she meet if he were alone with her in some distant place?

Therefore she betrayed his thoughts to Ain and asked her to hide her betrayal. Ain wondered sadly, "Where would he find a house like ours? But he has come to hate the neighborhood!"

For the first time she thought about modernizing the structure of her historic house. She spent liberally to provide it with water, sewers, and electricity, to the point that Ezzat marveled at her sudden decision. She asked, laughingly, "Why not? The world is changing, and there are innovations that are beneficial and do no harm." Then she added, after a little while, "Does modern furniture appeal to you?"

He asked listlessly, "What does it matter?"

"You're young and the young have their tastes. Possibly you could bring new pieces and place them among the old, and possibly we could redo your room completely, why not? What do you like?"

He shrugged his shoulders without speaking. He was seized by the suspicion that Sayyida had betrayed him, and he asked her when they were alone, "Did you let her know about my desire to leave?"

She denied it strongly, but he said scornfully, "A gossip and a traitor like your mother!"

Ain learned of the quarrel and confronted him with the candor she preferred. She said to him, "Don't torment Umm Samir anymore. This is your house and I have modernized it for your sake. If you want to live independently far from your neighborhood I won't oppose your wishes. You have complete freedom, so do as you please."

Thus he found himself free—once again—with no impediments. His ambition quickly languished and his hesitation stirred.

As usual he stopped on the threshold. Wherever did this paralysis come from? Was it from his own life, which had turned into sleepy stupidity? Did Ain have some secret which he still didn't know?

11

Ain appeared to him one morning with eyes red from weeping, alarming him greatly. He did not remember seeing her cry before. With a sinking heart, he asked her what was wrong, expecting the worst. She whispered, in a sad voice, "Baraka's gone. . . . God preserve you!"

He couldn't help but smile, feeling he had been saved, and stammered, "Cats fill the house, may your life be preserved."

"But Baraka was the origin, her heart was filled with love and good sense. There was no escaping it, her time had come."

He had become accustomed to this spiritualism, accepting the fact of the communion between his mother and the cats and linking it with her vitality, undiminished after seventy years. Likewise he had become accustomed to unexciting intimacy with Sayyida; in fact he suffered when she miscarried twice for no apparent reason, and his heart skipped a beat when his mother said to him one day, "The time has come for us to send Samir to Sheikh al-Azizi!"

It was true, Samir was now six, and Ain's features were clear in his face. Time progressed; Ezzat was twenty-five, and nothing outwardly important had happened during that time. But a hidden change had occurred, which he revealed to no one.

A wonderful and alarming change. It was the lassitude that seeped into his religious feelings. It was not related to any of the patrons of the hashish den, for they were believers. The crime novels had nothing to do with it, and thinking had no part in the matter because he did not think. It was just that lassitude had extinguished his ardor and conviction, so that the pillars of the temple had collapsed. He desisted from prayer and fasting but he kept that to himself, so no one was aware of it. The world became empty and it was beyond his power to reanimate it, this world of emptiness and lies.

Ramadan al-Zaini, the elder of the hashish den, noticed his gloom one night and said to him, "If you count God's blessings you cannot number them."

He smiled questioningly, and the man said, "Rank and money and youth, what more do you want?"

The man spoke truly. Even if he came into his inheritance, what more would he do than he was doing now?

The den was located in a unique place, on the border separating history and our era, in a watchtower in the ancient fort standing atop the old tunnel. In times past it had been the northern gate of Cairo, and the fort had been the center of security and defense. Today the fort was yet another monument, the tunnel was a passageway and a place where beggars slept, and Ramadan al-Zaini was the one who had chosen the surveillance tower as the place for the den. It was neither too large nor too small, and it was well ventilated by a window from which archers had shot their arrows. He made the official watchman into a servant for the gathering, preparing the water pipe and passing it around, and sharing in the smoking and the supper.

Ezzat celebrated Samir's starting the kuttab by presenting the party with a grilled lamb and a tray of sweet basbusa. It was an unforgettable night, not only for the happy occasion but also because of news brought by Ramadan al-Zaini. He said, "Yesterday I saw something no eye has seen."

The drowsy eyes looked up at him, and he said, "The Lawandi Circus was in Darb al-Ahmar so I went to see it. The show began with a play, and I saw an actress and an actor. Who do you think they were?"

A voice said jokingly, "Your mother and father."

But he continued, taking no notice, "Badriya al-Manawishi and Hamdoun Agrama!"

People clamored, "No way."

As for Ezzat, a bucket of ice water had spilled over his head. He opened his half-closed eyes and saw the past, embodied and clothed in violent emotions.

Pleased by the interest he had aroused, Ramadan said, "In the flesh."

"What a scandal!"

Ramadan said, "What begins with elopement ends in the circus."

Poisonous comments flew, and the past came back to Ezzat as if it hadn't left him for a single moment, let alone seven full

53

years or more. In spite of himself he stammered, "What an end!"

Ramadan said, "I made up my mind to embarrass him, so I went to greet him."

"He must have been embarrassed!"

"Not at all. . . . He laughed. . . . He welcomed me. He is recklessness itself."

Ezzat asked him, "Is the circus still performing in Darb al-Ahmar?"

"Not at all. . . . But Hamdoun promised to visit us here."

"Impossible."

"You'll see for yourselves in a little while."

"He really is outrageous."

Ezzat was troubled. Would he really see Hamdoun in a little while? What did it matter? The past had been erased and love had died as friendship had died, but the sudden leap of the past into the present didn't pass without shock. His imagination pictured the meeting in multiple ways but what happened in fact was different from what he had imagined, for no sooner did Ezzat see Hamdoun looking at him from under his prominent eyebrows, smiling radiantly and opening his arms, than he answered the invitation and embraced him warmly. Hamdoun whispered in his ear, "I only came because of you, when I heard that you were one of the regulars here."

He quickly began to share in the smoking, spontaneously and without embarrassment. No one found the courage to attack him, though Ramadan said, "I never imagined I would find you in a circus."

He replied, laughing, "Our work is limited to the play, and it's one of my compositions."

"But you were a government employee."

"I still am. Theater is a hobby, nothing more."

"But. . . ."

Ramadan didn't finish, so Hamdoun laughed and said, "But my wife, isn't that it? She's an artist like me, though there's no use trying to convince our neighborhood of that. But we are an honorable family like other honorable families."

There was no sound but the gurgle of the water pipe. Then he looked at Ezzat and said, "It's a pleasure to share in celebrating your son's entering the kuttab."

"And you, how many children do you have?"

"I had one who didn't live more than a year, and nothing after that. Praise God."

Ramadan asked him, "Wouldn't you like to have children?"

"They would get in way of our artistic work!"

Once again the water pipe gurgled alone.

They left the den together. Ezzat invited him to his house, plunged in slumber. They sat in the garden despite the autumn chill at dawn. They exchanged true affection, without either of them referring to the past by a single word. Ezzat felt his spirit revive again. He seized on the friendship, pure after the painful memories had vanished. They returned to what had been, without a failed love to separate them. It was a miraculous tale worth telling. Hamdoun began to talk about his experiences, "I still have my government job, but my struggle for the sake of art hasn't faltered for a moment. I also discovered Badriya's talent, but how can we make our way over rocky ground? The theaters refused me as a writer and refused my wife as an actress. I did not despair. I met the owner of the Lawandi Circus and suggested to him that we present a one-act play instead of the crude slapstick. We didn't ask to be paid so he agreed to try it. We succeeded and the audience enjoyed it much more."

Ezzat said, "But a circus!"

"Yes, better than nothing until the future smiles on us."

Moved by pride, he told him about the commercial enterprise he was thinking of, and Hamdoun said, "There's no way around it, otherwise what is the meaning of life?"

"So your life now has a meaning?"

"It's filled with activity. Who knows, I might form a troupe some day."

"Can you stand up to the big theaters?"

"I mean a small troupe working in Rod al-Farag during the summer, and if we find any encouragement we'll work in the Egyptian Club during the winter—that's what I aspire to."

Ezzat's head spun, beset suddenly by strange ideas. He was invaded by an inspiration that reinvigorated his heart and will. Never before had he felt anything like the power he felt at that moment to create, to work, and to embark on something new. In order to prove to himself that he was awake and not dreaming he said, "Hamdoun, tell me about what you would have to spend."

The young man replied, interested, "Money for the theater and the actors and costumes and scenery. It's not an outlandish sum, but it shouldn't be less than five hundred pounds."

Ezzat thought for a while and then asked, "Is success guaranteed?"

"I think so, especially if we run the concession on our own account."

Silence reigned, filled with emotions, hope, and hidden motives. At last Ezzat murmured, "Let me think for a while, Hamdoun."

12

He did not really need to think (as the narrator says) for he was swept by a vital impulse, a strong and powerful outburst which made a new man of him, moving crazily, summoned by some deep call to action and rising against lassitude to the point that he didn't recognize himself, considering the matter sacred play, a happy game by which he would realize himself in a splendid way. It did not escape his notice that the new project must be enveloped in secrecy. It was neither something about which he could come to an understanding openly with Ain, nor something recognized and respected in the neighborhood; tongues would wag if the secret were discovered, liberally bestowing on him the ugliest epithets. That did not diminish his ambition, but rather it may have redoubled his enthusiasm and rebellion. Owner and manager of a theater; what might that mean? Stranger than that was that he did not find in himself any real interest in the theater; rather he was running after the unknown and its mysterious challenges, drawn to a fleeting moment that was filled with riches. There was no question that management suited him. Hamdoun's company amused him, the change of atmosphere from one extreme to the other enchanted him, and it was good to plunge into the experience free from the weakness of love and pain of self-delusion, with an alert and daring heart.

But would he encounter an unexpected obstacle in his mother? She had said to him, "It's a considerable sum, but it's yours gladly. I only want to know your project."

"A contracting company."

"Let me sit for an hour with your partners."

He quivered with rage, and shouted, "I'm not a minor, and these are men's affairs!"

She laughed and said, "May good fortune be your ally."

Hamdoun accompanied him to his old apartment on Muhammad Ali Street to have lunch. When the dwelling appeared to him he felt a strong urge to flee, although the desire hastened off in one direction while he continued in the other, arm in arm with Hamdoun. In a moment or so he would see Badriya al-Manawishi, actress in the Lawandi Circus, and touch the palm of her hand for the first time in his life. If that had happened seven years before, he would have been electrified or set ablaze, but he went today liberated, the old lover having dissolved in the current of time, his place taken by another who dreamed of management, command, and innocent amusement.

The door opened on her glowing countenance and sweet smile. She was wearing a dress dotted with white, and the old voice returned in lively greeting, "Welcome . . . welcome. . . ."

He entered a new world from which there was no turning back. He had had to search for it among the ruins of the past, and here he was invading it blessed with health and friendship. He remembered the pain of love and was amazed. He sat in a modest living room as they immersed themselves in courtesies and neutral memories, then he was called to the table. The furnishings of the house spoke of poverty; his friend was suffering, and here he was coming at the appropriate time. He began to eat with enthusiasm, saying, "I have learned how to eat as one should."

Badriya said, "You have gained weight, perhaps more than you should."

Hamdoun objected, "It is very appropriate for the owner and director of a theater."

Badriya replied, "Here are the baked eggplant and grape leaves, which Hamdoun has told me you like."

In the living room again, Ezzat said to Hamdoun, "I hope you have used your time well."

Hamdoun answered confidently, "We will begin on the first day of the summer season. I have chosen the actors and actresses and the rest of the workers, and this after-noon Ustaz Yousif Radi, the lawyer, is coming. Everything is ready."

He remembered the death of her father years earlier and offered his condolences. He asked, "Do you see your mother?"

She answered shortly, "She married some time ago and moved permanently to al-Ballina."

Hamdoun said laughing, "It's nice for a man to live without a mother-in-law."

Badriya said to him, "You're a writer and a rascal."

"What's important is to succeed as a writer. . . . Would you like to see my library?"

Ezzat answered listlessly, "Of course, but later on."

Badriya asked, "How is Sitt Ain? Is she still showering kindness on the people of the neighborhood?"

He answered coldly, "With great energy and activity."

"I think the time has come for her to rest."

"She's still young!"

Hamdoun said sincerely, "She deserves eternal honor."

Ezzat laughed, "Sometimes I think we're a family of madmen!"

"Then madness is the best prescription for saving the world."

"Do you still think the world needs saving?"

Hamdoun raised his hands to heaven and cried, "As God is my witness!"

Ezzat noticed that Badriya's cheer disappeared suddenly and that she changed the course of the conversation, saying, "I wouldn't have agreed to drag you into our project unless I was sure your money wouldn't be wasted."

"It's really amazing that you are succeeding as an actress."

She motioned to Hamdoun and said, "It's because of him; he discovered me and he's my teacher. He drills me on my lines, and insisted on improving my reading so I can memorize by myself."

Hamdoun said, "That's not important as long as we present comic pieces, but I dream of presenting Shakespeare's plays in translation, so you will have to improve your pronunciation of formal Arabic."

"Laughter guarantees success; the manager will support my opinion."

Ezzat smiled but refused to join the conversation, so Hamdoun said, "Tears succeed like laughter, and the lady has given an excellent reading of scenes from *Julius Caesar*."

At first he forgot the neighborhood completely, as if it were a mythical memory; then Sayyida came to sit beside Badriya and invite a harsh comparison. The same upbringing in the neighborhood and the kuttab. This one sparkles with intelligence, beauty, and enterprise, while the other hides behind a cunning humility with her dark complexion, her rounded nose, and her impenetrable submission. But what had Hamdoun done with Badriya and what had he done with Sayyida? He also said that Sayyida had given birth to Samir while this beauty had given birth to nothing. If her destiny had been to marry him the fates would have been different, for better or for worse.

The best thing to do was not to think about anything except his new position as a manager for these two stars, with which he was very happy. Borne on a rising tide of enthusiasm, he said, "Perhaps we can rent a large theater in the future."

Hamdoun spread his legs and leaned back on the sofa to give free reign to his dreams. As for Badriya, she said, "The important thing is to succeed at first."

Ezzat muttered, "If she gave me what she squanders on other people, if I were to sell a single apartment building!"

Hamdoun sat up and protested, "I object to dreams that aren't innocent."

Ezzat said, without any obvious connection, "I would like to have a place of my own, far from the neighborhood."

In mid-afternoon the apartment doorbell rang. Hamdoun rose to answer it, saying, "Ustaz Yousif Radi has come, and the work begins."

13

Winter and early spring brought about arrangements, preparations, and money spent, just as they brought about a close friendship among Ezzat, Hamdoun, and Badriya. The narrator considers that this was among the happiest times in the life of Ezzat Abdel Baqi. He spent a large portion of it in Hamdoun's apartment, where contracts were written with the theater's owner, the actors and the actresses, the technicians and the workers. He had renovated parts of the theater building, providing it with new seats and setting up a new entrance so that it became the gem of Rod al-Farag, in the words of Amm Farag Ya Musahhil, the janitor and barker, who was from the neighborhood. In April they transferred the work to the theater itself, where Ezzat liked the manager's office with its large desk, the safe, and the comfortable leather chairs, and performed his work as manager and theater owner. Being in command was not a strange situation for him, but it had not previously extended to others of this sort. The actresses looked very vulgar in his eyes, nearer to the world of prostitution than to the world of art, and it seemed to him that they vied with each other in offering themselves to him. He began to prepare an apartment of his own in a middle-sized house in Shubra Gardens, where he intended to summon his own family after taking advantage of it for himself. Hamdoun noticed his sexual interests and said to him, "Listen to your friend: They are all cheap, as you see; real actresses don't abandon their theaters for one like ours. Any relationship you have with one of these women will detract from your position as manager. Do what you like, but not here."

He took the advice, finding no great difficulty but also no real desire. He dedicated himself to his work with energy and passion, or rather the new man dedicated himself to it, the one who had been created on the night of the celebration for Samir's entry into the kuttab. At midnight he would join Ramadan al-Zaini's den in the watchtower in the ruins of the ancient fort, then he would move on to Ain's house at daybreak.

As manager, he read the text of the play *The Sultan's Companion*, adapted from *The Thousand and One Nights*, which was one Hamdoun had produced from his growing store of writings. He also watched the rehearsals, observing Hamdoun as he undertook the numerous duties of producing a play, and he stared with amazement at Badriya as she strutted in the costume of a Byzantine slave girl. It was regrettable that he had no role in this complicated, magical, enchanting work. Hamdoun said to him, "There will be stiff competition; there are three theaters in addition to ours."

Badriya answered, "Our advantage is that our play is new; their plays are all revivals taken from the comic repertory."

Ustaz Yousif Radi said, "Don't forget that they change the show every week. This place won't support a single play more than two or three weeks, even if it's new!"

Hamdoun said, "I have plenty, and we have the classics also."

The lawyer answered, "I also have a new play!"

Badriya asked him, "Comedy?"

"A serious drama dealing with the problem of polygamy."

Hamdoun said, "A subject suitable for comic treatment also."

"But I approached it from its tragic side."

Badriya said, "It's not suitable for Rod al-Farag in any case."

Yousif Radi looked pleadingly at Ezzat and the latter said, with new confidence, "Let me read it first."

He was comfortable with the decision and considered it at the heart of his work.

The opening night was the first of May. Amm Farag Ya Musahhil stood in front of the entrance, shouting in a ringing voice, "Here . . . the artist Sitt Badriya . . . a new play never before performed . . . *The Sultan's Companion* . . . laughter until midnight . . . songs and dance . . . drinks of all kinds. . . ."

Ezzat's nerves were tense. He had not known this state before except in the ordeal of love, and when he neglected his devotions for the first time. During the period of preparation he had watched the stars of the competing troupes and his mind was at rest about Badriya's superiority, but he did not laugh—as he had expected—when he followed the rehearsals of *The Sultan's Companion*. He had leaned toward Ustaz Yousif Radi (the two were alone in the seats for the audience) and whispered in surprise, "There's nothing funny!"

The lawyer answered, seizing the opportunity, "We are in the time of drama and tears!"

His heart sank at that, and he wondered if he would return to his mother penniless! For that reason his nerves were tense as opening day dawned, but the audience was the largest one of all, and the theaters were packed with patrons. The concession worked beyond its capacity, as bottles of soda and ginger ale and sandwiches of fuul, falafel, and bastirma were consumed by the dozens. Moreover, the audience roared with laughter and vied with each other in showing their appreciation for Badriya by expressions that went beyond the bounds of decency in many instances. The show's success was clear to him; he regained his confidence and pride, his appreciation of Hamdoun redoubled, and he joined the audience in its pleasure, even though he was seeing the play for the tenth time.

14

After they finished around midnight, Badriya and Hamdoun came to his room with happy faces, and he congratulated them on their success. Hamdoun said enthusiastically, "Success beyond all expectations."

Badriya stammered, "Now that God has saved us from the circus."

Ezzat stood, saying, "We'll celebrate our success in Shubra Gardens!"

Badriya, Hamdoun, and Yousif Radi gathered in the new apartment, as well as Farag Ya Musahhil, who served them. Kebabs, pistachios, and whiskey were brought while Farag Ya Musahhil devoted himself to preparing the water pipe. Ezzat tasted whiskey for the first time in his life, and he was invaded by a new sense of rapture, for he no longer cared about his strange situation or the deterioration of his values. He saw the glass in Badriya's hand and was possessed by the feeling that they—all of them—were foreigners, and that the old neighborhood had been a dream, nothing more. Hamdoun became intoxicated and declaimed, "I met Ezzat in the kuttab of Sheikh al-Azizi, and there on the mat an eternal friendship was created. But I didn't know until this moment that we were destined to share a single fate."

Ezzat said, "Every man has a true family for whom he was created, and when he finds his way to it his true life begins."

Badriya cried, "We had to wander for a long time before we found our way to ourselves!"

Ezzat abandoned himself to a marvelous inspiration, which opened his heart to a dazzling illumination. He loved everything with fantastic force. At the same time, it would have been easier for him to part with heart or liver than to part with Hamdoun, Badriya, and the theater that led the way to their eternal union. He said that there were unimagined treasures of joy in the world. But anyone who desires happiness must be decisive with the obstacles shrouded in the darkness of ancient recesses. He said, "I would like to sing, if it weren't for the ugliness of my voice!"

Hamdoun answered laughing, "Let's leave that to your conscience."

Badriya said, pointing to Hamdoun, "He used to wake up often, saying, I dreamed of Ezzat!"

Ezzat asked, "What did you dream?"

"Ah . . . how fast we forget our dreams!"

Badriya said, "But I still remember a dream he told me about. He dreamed he saw the two of you dancing together on a boat."

"I wonder what the interpretation is."

"He doesn't care about that!"

Farag Ya Musahhil said, "It has come true in our theater 'Paradise,' because it is a boat on the banks of the Nile."

They quickly welcomed the interpretation, although Ezzat wondered to himself, what was I dreaming at that time?

On his way to the neighborhood he felt very resentful and cursed the compulsory movements that closed the circle. Even the patrons of the hashish den had found their way to bed. As he plunged through the darkness he collided with a well-known lunatic who liked to wander in the dark. The man's head fell against him as he muttered long, drawn-out words with no meaning, and his saliva flowed over Ezzat's cheek and neck. The young man was disgusted and gave him a hard shove, sending him sprawling on his back, howling. At a distance he heard the sound of the watchman clearing his throat, inquiring and warning, and the coercion reached its limit. A decision sprang from him, fully formed in every dimension, with no prior planning. Like a highwayman springing from his ambush. To turn back, forever. To jump from the battlements of the ancient fort in pursuit of a new fate.

He turned on his heel and went reeling on his way, drunk with overpowering joy.

The narrator says:

The following afternoon a messenger came to Ain's house bearing papers attesting Ezzat's divorce from Sayyida. Sayyida broke into tears and began to gather her clothes in a flood of emotion. Ain rested her head against the back of the sofa, decorated with sayings and maxims, and closed her eyes. She began to whisper, "How right you are, my heart!"

When she opened her eyes she saw Sayyida finishing gathering her clothes and Samir watching her anxiously. Ain cried, "What's this?"

She sat up and said in a tone of command, "Put your clothes back where they go."

Sayyida said in an unsteady voice, "How can I stay with him under one roof?"

Ain answered sadly, "He will not return to us again."

She stood and paced the room, muttering, "I would not be surprised if the roof turned into a cloud and rain poured down from it."

66

Sayyida stammered, "Let me go to my mother."

Ain answered in exasperation, "I have told you that I am your mother. This is your house, and this is your son, Samir. Stay here until God gives you someone better."

She put the clothes back with her own hands, continuing, "My heart told me that something would happen. Clouds do not gather to no purpose."

She took Samir by the hand to the sofa and said to him, changing her tone, "Sheikh al-Azizi has praised you highly. Work hard and comfort our wounded hearts."

The boy whispered anxiously, "Papa . . ."

"He has traded us for dirt, that is your father!"

She wondered, disturbed, "Why shouldn't deeds be repaid in kind?"

Then she sighed, and addressed the unknown, "I brought him up as well as I could, I blessed him with guidance and love; what's wrong with him? He always seemed to be eager to travel —where? Why do you quarrel with the air and defy peace of mind? Why do you go looking for trouble?"

Life continued at its deliberate pace in the house and the neighborhood. Sayyida stayed in the house, her new life free of fighting. Ain resumed her rounds dispensing love and mercy, showing steadfastness and noble patience in the face of troubles. She took pleasure in Samir's hard work and progress. Ezzat's news spread throughout the neighborhood—divorce and abandonment—and men and women both cursed the prodigal son.

15

The season passed successfully. The Paradise troupe presented four plays written by Hamdoun. At the end of August new activity began, to prepare the Egyptian Club for the winter season. Ezzat became adept at his profession of manager; he longed to see Samir but he did not think of visiting the neighborhood at all. A discussion of the new season took place in Ezzat's office, in which Hamdoun Agrama said, "I caution you against Yousif Radi's play."

Ezzat answered, "I'll find some way to convince him."

At that Badriya wondered, "Will we present our comic plays in the Egyptian Club?"

Hamdoun answered, "They aren't comic in the usual sense, since I use comedy to say things that have their own value."

Ezzat said, "Great, but you've often talked to me about another plan."

"If we must be serious we have the translations of Shakespeare's plays."

Badriya inclined her head gracefully, and said sweetly, "I love *Julius Caesar*!"

Ezzat saw the movement of the head and heard the voice, and something happened. He was indifferent to the rest of the conversation. They bade him farewell and left without his knowledge. Alone, he stammered, "My God . . . I love her!"

She was the whole of his heart and soul and life. Had the old love been resurrected in that moment? Or had it never gone away? Had it been toying with him the whole time? It was a splendid, frightening thing. It took life by storm and freighted the future with multiple possibilities. In any case, it had swept away peace forever. The problem of Yousif Radi receded into the background. Yes, his relationship with him had become close; it was thanks to him that he had met some of his girlfriends. He had lit up nights of debauchery in Ezzat's apartment, but he had not enjoyed them as he had imagined. Commercial love seemed to him disgusting in the extreme. Something hidden in his nature spoiled his peace of mind and filled him with anxiety and aversion. Something hidden, enamored of contrariness, even before he discovered his love. Or before he admitted it: he became intensely clear to himself, as fish become clear swimming just below the surface of transparent water. Who knew, perhaps he had risked embarking on his new life, perhaps he had abandoned Ain and Samir and Sayyida and the neighborhood only because of her, because of Badriya, and in pursuit of her unknown call.

Now he was a prisoner completely, his life besieged by unknown enemies. When would the explosion happen? But easy does it. Things must be dealt with in a different fashion. Let the love remain a secret buried under friendship and work. Let life continue in its sweetness and let its hidden torments subside. The old contradiction he had suffered under his mother's wing returned to him. He loved Badriya and resented her. He loved Hamdoun and abhorred him. He was blessed by success and in the iron grip of anxiety. In addition to all of that he had to deal with her—Badriya—innocently and spontaneously. But his self-confidence was shaken, exposed to the blowing winds of fear. And she—this was certain—loved her husband to the point of adoration. It seemed that she was faithful and upright by nature. Her attitude toward her many fans was proverbial. How stupid his neighborhood was to accuse her and her husband. Stupid people accused him of trading in his wife's honor. Would that he had been someone of that sort. Then life would have taken a course of singular harmony and happiness.

What stirred him most strongly was the hour of sleeplessness, sometimes, at the end of the night. He would awaken floating in an ethereal world, his breast seething with the deepest emotions of grief and sadness. How terrible the hours of sleeplessness, when torrents of gleaming images would rain down on him from the clouds of memory, spreading out in tears and blood and darkness and moaning. At that point he would return to the earliest primitiveness, imbued with innocence, savagery, and mysteries. He began to steal time from watching eyes under the cover of darkness, standing in a corner to watch her role on the stage in intimacy and supplication, wondering in terror what fate would be the result of this madness.

The narrator says:

A few days before the end of the season events plunged into a new, unexpected course, upsetting their balance and quickening their pace, taking off like a missile.

Ezzat was in the manager's office when Badriya came in alone, an hour or so before curtain time.

Even though she seemed uneasy and distracted, still his heart beat with deep delight, for it was the first time he had been alone with her since he began working with her. She sat, saying in an apologetic tone, "I'm forced to share my personal concerns with you."

His delight doubled at the confidence placed in him by the one he loved most. He said, "Your concerns are mine also."

She brought her head so close to the desk that a lock of her black hair touched its glass cover, and she whispered, "There is one thing that unites us in these concerns."

He stammered, controlling his emotions with great difficulty, "You have my complete attention."

"That thing is our love for Hamdoun!"

He retreated until the back of his head collided with the wall of cold reality. He said, "Of course."

"Strange things are happening in our house which might threaten our life, our work, and our future."

"What might these strange things be?"

"Have you heard of Tomorrow's Children?

"Yes."

"Some of them sneak into my apartment from under the arcade every night."

"How?"

"After we come back from the theater and the police are sleeping, or so they think!"

"I barely understand anything."

"They are rebels against everything, and they are wanted."

"And accused of known assassinations!"

"That is the issue."

"Do you mean that Hamdoun . . . ?"

He took refuge in silence and she said, sighing, "Yes. I thought it was only a matter of heartfelt sympathy until they chose our apartment as a meeting place. In vain I tried to prevent that, not to mention trying to convince him to leave them."

Ezzat thought about it, stammering, "It really is a dangerous thing."

"That's why I'm coming to you."

He asked in confusion, "You mean I should bring up the subject with him?"

"Do you have any other idea?"

"Won't he be angry with you for betraying his secret?"

She answered quickly, "He must not know that!"

"Then how will I explain my knowledge of it to him?"

"I don't know. . . . But keep suspicion away from me!"

She looked at her wristwatch and got up, saying, "I rely on God, and then on you."

Quickly she left the room.

16

She left him in a vortex, a vortex that allowed no part of him to remain in its natural place. The world was colors and sounds and thoughts and angels and devils colliding with each other, drunken confidence, readiness to help. He sat confused for a long time. An unknown joy passed over him. He had to find his way to an idea. The picture of Hamdoun came to his mind, Hamdoun dressed in prison clothes or on the gallows. He said aloud to himself that there must be a plan to rescue the situation. Badriya could not be abandoned or widowed, she could not.

He must think the best of Hamdoun. He must not neglect his duty. Fate did not neglect its duty, either.

At the end of the night before the last one in the season, Ezzat said to Hamdoun, "I would like to celebrate our success in your apartment, just the three of us!"

Hamdoun Agrama was startled, and said, "I'm not my best tonight!"

"The whiskey will refresh you."

He asked hesitatingly, "Isn't your apartment better for our purpose?"

"But it's not empty!"

"Let us see your beautiful new sweetheart!"

Ezzat wondered, indignantly, "It's as if you don't want me there?"

They had hardly settled in their seats when the bell rang. Hamdoun hurried to the door. Within minutes he returned, his tension gone. Ezzat raised his glass, saying, "Your health . . . a visitor at this hour of the night?"

Hamdoun answered, laughing, "Someone who lost his way in the dark!"

He took a drink, moving his eyes from one to the other, then stammered, "Don't try to deceive me."

"Deceive you?"

"Don't try to deceive me."

Badriya asked, "What?"

Ezzat said, with a frightening calm, "You have both been accused."

Hamdoun cried, his face going pale, "Tell us frankly what's on your mind."

He answered tersely and confidently, "Tomorrow's Children!"

Hamdoun's face grew paler, and Badriya averted her eyes. Hamdoun said, "I don't understand."

"On the contrary, you understand everything."

A silence like death descended, but it did not linger long, as Ezzat said, "What danger you are exposing yourselves to!"

Hamdoun asked with concern, "Who told you?"

"Someone I trust."

"Damn him!"

"Who do you mean? You don't know him. . . . If I weren't sure I can trust him I would urge you to flee."

"Yousif Radi!"

"Certainly not."

"He and none other."

"I told you no and I swear it! How would he know?"

"He's with us in another group but he thinks I steal the spotlight from his genius!"

"I swear to you that it's another person."

"Who is it?"

"I'm not in a position to give his name. I will tell you some day when he frees me from my oath. That's not important. How did you two get involved in this?"

Hamdoun answered with irritation, "She has nothing to do with it."

Badriya said, "I'm only interested in the theater."

Ezzat said to Hamdoun, "If only you were like that."

"I can't help it."

"All your life you've concerned yourself with things that don't matter to anyone."

"Don't matter to anyone?"

"I won't argue with you about that, I only want to know if these suspicious meetings will continue."

Hamdoun took refuge in silence and Ezzat said, "We are friends and more than brothers, with a shared life. We are barely beginning, and you have a bright future. You can't marry art and crime—you have to save yourself before it's too late to repent."

He returned to Shubra Gardens saying to himself, "I never imagined that angels and devils could live next to each other in the same country!"

17

At the height of the vortex the next night—closing night—he saw his aunt Amouna, her daughter Ihsan, and an unknown young man entering the theater. Their eyes met, so he went to greet her. It was a lukewarm encounter, but he met his cousin's new husband, who had invited his mother-in-law to join them in an outing as part of their honeymoon celebrations. He realized that the truth of his new profession would become known in the house and the neighborhood, and that tongues would wag with this fine story. From time to time he had been toying with the idea of visiting the family, but he had turned away from it decisively, despite his longing to see Samir. The old Ezzat Abdel Baqi had ended and in his place appeared a man inclining to stoutness, practicing his profession in a milieu shrouded in suspicion. He would content himself with charging Amm Farag Ya Musahhil—who hailed from the neighborhood—with inquiring about the news and telling him how things stood.

The fifteenth of October was set as the opening night for the winter season at the Egyptian Club. The success of the summer season infused him with confidence, but the future nonetheless seemed obscure to him; the depths of his heart, where love was fused with terrifying fantasies, made him uneasy and apprehensive. In that period he was alone with Badriya only for a moment, and he asked her, "How are you?"

"The meetings have stopped, but. . . ."

"But?"

"But Hamdoun is in bad shape."

He said to himself that it was good that the meetings had ended, although he smiled mockingly. There was an importunate image in his mind, the image of Hamdoun in prison clothes, always accompanied by a feeling of pain hissing from the secret voice that spoiled his peace of mind.

Yousif Radi said to him, "It would be fitting to open the season with my play."

Ezzat answered amiably, "We will do that one day."

The young man replied, "I'm thinking about inviting Hamdoun someday to listen to his opinion and make the changes he thinks are necessary."

"That's the best thing to do."

In Hamdoun's apartment, they compared *Julius Caesar* and *The Sultan's Companion* as to which would be better for the opening. Badriya said, "*Julius Caesar* is terrific but my part in it is trivial."

Hamdoun said, "You've memorized Anthony's lines out of appreciation and love, so maybe it would be a novelty to have you play his role."

Ezzat cried, "The role of a man?"

"Why not? It would be an exciting surprise."

Nothing was decided in the meeting, but events moved with astonishing speed. The next day the lifeless body of Yousif Radi was discovered in a small apartment in al-Qubaisi where he lived alone. The newspapers published the news with a picture, describing the crime as savage and mysterious.

Ezzat trembled, and the arena of his mind turned into a terrifying theater of shadows. He and the devil were the only ones who knew the secret. He found the devil crouching in his innermost depths, pointing laughingly to Hamdoun. Hamdoun, who had killed an innocent man for an imaginary crime he had not committed. Who killed Yousif Radi? It wasn't Hamdoun only, rather he—Ezzat—was behind it, and Badriya also. You really are a dangerous man, Hamdoun, but you're finished. You're finished. Finished. Finished. Today or tomorrow or the day after. Sir. You are the one who started the friendship in the kuttab. You are destiny and God's decree. You are the miracle man. Esteemed sir. Where can I get away from that voice pursuing me and spoiling my peace of mind? What was the sin of the innocent man who was killed in treachery and ignorance? How long will the devil stick to me, laughing? Esteemed sir. A chance. There's a chance of atonement. There's a chance of madness. There's a chance of torment. There's a chance of love. Let us stand before the scales of judgment. Your honor. Who are you that you should litigate, prosecute, and judge? Who are you that you should execute also? You always issue a death sentence for others. You did that twice. Each time the unseen crier calls for an eye for an eye. That I bear the burden of my offense is justice. That I bear the offense of others is madness. Even if being did not emerge from nothingness it's still a hopeless experiment. The devil's laughter must be stopped or else his guffaws will shake the walls. What might Ain be thinking about at this moment in time? Don't let time get away from you. Your Honor the Prosecutor General.

18

Outwardly, preparations for the new season continued, but the killing of Yousif Radi had been a violent shock for everyone. All the members of the troupe knew him personally. The preparer of contracts and anticipated playwright. He was killed yesterday and the investigation examined every angle. They were all questioned and nothing was discovered. Hamdoun went with them. Ezzat did not disclose any of his anxieties. He returned in the company of Hamdoun and Badriya. Hamdoun kept silent the whole time.

Ezzat said, lamenting, "What a shame!"

Hamdoun continued, "Yes, he was young."

As women usually do, Badriya sobbed. The world seemed strange, as if it had been created anew but in a repulsive color. On their way they passed the mailbox that he had used yesterday for the first time. He wondered whether the letter had left it or was still waiting. Ezzat . . . Hamdoun . . . Badriya. The mailbox. What savagery, Badriya. When we find only the devil as a messenger to the vigilant conscience! I see Ain spreading her umbrella to protect herself from the sun's rays. I have the honor to inform your Excellency.

The afternoon of the same day Badriya stormed into his apartment in Shubra Gardens, an unexpected visit, obviously in misery and disarray, heralding dreadful things. The letter hadn't arrived yet, so what had gotten into her? She flung herself on a chair in the living room and closed her eyes in fatigue. He stood before her in shock, whispering, "Is everything all right? What happened to you?"

She stammered, clearly in despair, "It's ruin."

"Badriya . . . let out what's bothering you all at once."

She answered, sighing like someone drawing her last breath, "Hamdoun has gone mad, he divorced me, he beat me, he went to confess to the crime of killing Yousif Radi."

Pretending to be distressed while the world around him came apart and flew in all directions, he cried, "What madness!"

"It's the truth!"

He saw an ugliness in her face without knowing where it came from; he saw another woman. He said, "I want to understand before I go mad myself!"

She looked away from him and said, as if she were confessing to someone unknown, "I've been in turmoil ever since I learned of Yousif Radi's killing. My suspicions went to Hamdoun; I realized the man was a victim of a crime he did not commit. I was stricken with terror and the dreadful feeling that I was the true killer."

"That means I'm a partner, but it's all pure delusion."

"It's not delusion at all. I think you have shared the same torment. After we returned to the house Hamdoun noticed my complete transformation. I couldn't bear it any longer and I told him the truth about my fear that Yousif Radi had been a victim of a crime he didn't commit."

Ezzat said sadly, "You rushed in without thinking."

"The confession escaped me when I was miserable, in a state of collapse."

"How did he take that?"

"His face went dark, he asked precisely what I meant. I confessed to him that Yousif Radi did not betray the secret of the meetings to you and that I was the one who did it!"

Ezzat scowled, his face becoming hidden under a rough mask of gloom. She seemed drawn to a terrifying, tyrannical memory. Then she said, "You can't imagine what happened. He sprang from his seat as if he had been stung, his face took on a bloodthirsty look, he slapped me so hard I nearly lost consciousness, he accused me of the crime, and in my pain I turned the accusation back on him. I yelled: It's you who killed him!"

Ezzat moaned, asking, "Is this the reward of someone moved by goodwill to save the one he loves?"

"He began hitting the wall with his fist, threatening disaster, he threw divorce in my face, he kept on howling like a wounded beast. Then he focused his eyes on me fully and said with pure loathing: You are hellfire, and as for me, I'm finished."

"He threw on his clothes and left the apartment, saying: I'll divorce you first, then I'll give myself up."

Ezzat cried, "What misery!"

Badriya broke into tears and said, "He left me in a terrifying loneliness."

He was clothed in the same terrifying loneliness. Why had he rushed to write the anonymous letter? It was as if he had no goal other than to attest his own baseness. Hamdoun was going to confess a day or two before the letter arrived. It was absurd to try to convince himself that he had done what his duty as a man dictated. Here Badriya was free and Hamdoun was in shackles, hadn't that been his urgent dream? But he was sick and Badriya was ugly. The world was seriously anemic and not fit for love. Sorrowfully, he said, "Wash your face, drink a cup of tea, we have to think calmly about the disaster."

She got up, moaning, and said, "He doesn't know how much I love him!"

19

It was now known that Hamdoun Agrama, the author and actor, was the killer of the lawyer Yousif Radi, and that the motive for the crime was that the killer had noticed the victim's infatuation with his wife. News also spread of the anonymous letter which accused Hamdoun of killing Yousif. Badriya was interrogated again and she confirmed what Hamdoun said and did not make the slightest reference to the group Tomorrow's Children. In her terrifying solitude Badriya found no companion or supporter other than Ezzat. Her sudden ugliness disappeared, but her features were weighted with a deep, abiding grief; despite his own bitterness he did not lose hope in the near or distant future. The troupe continued rehearsals without Badriya's participation, rerunning the plays they had presented in Rod al-Farag. Ezzat intentionally let Badriya know from time to time that he was still carrying on his work as manager. Then too, she knew that he had no source of income other than his work. Thus he found the courage to say to her one day, "We must begin work on time, otherwise we will risk bankruptcy. . . ."

She mumbled, in deep distress, "How I hate it!"

"I feel the same way, but there's no way around it."

She said sadly, "We have no author now."

"But we have a considerable stock of plays, not to mention the classics and the translations."

"He's irreplaceable!"

"That's true, but we have to think about everything, and about the future."

At that point she said, hopefully, "There's something important I'd like to accomplish before the beginning of the season."

"You'll have all the help you expect from me and more."

"I've met with Hamdoun's lawyer and he gave me a lot of hope that he can be saved from hanging."

"I hope so, since he turned himself in and gave an extenuating excuse for the crime."

"I asked him to tell him how much I want him to marry me again!"

He didn't know what to say as he received this merciless new blow. As for Badriya, she continued, "That would help me go on living."

He answered listlessly, "That would be really great."

Ezzat prepared for the opening of the new season feeling that he was the most contemptible thing in existence. It did not relieve his feelings to learn later that Hamdoun had refused Badriya's request, in fact refusing even to see her. The season began with middling success, and he was well aware that Badriya had lost a lot of her theatrical magic. Days followed one another with no prospect of any good news, while Hamdoun's trial was concluded and he was sentenced to hard labor for life.

Farag Ya Musahhil came to him as usual with the news of the neighborhood, and said, on the subject of Hamdoun's sentence, "No one in the neighborhood sympathized with him!"

Ezzat answered sadly, "Maybe they are hoping for a similar fate for me!"

"Sitt Ain protects you from all ill will by her generosity with everyone."

"What's the news of the house?"

"The lady is as usual, she is who she is and doesn't change. Umm Samir refused to marry Alaish the carpenter, preferring to remain with her son, and Samir is progressing in his study with success and intelligence."

He remembered the garden, the hashish den in the historic fort, and Samir, who would grow up without knowing his father. But why was he thinking about the past, when his connections to it had been severed forever?

He said to Badriya, "What do you think about trying my luck with the late Yousif Radi's play?"

She said without enthusiasm, "Give it a try, the season up to now hasn't been very successful."

"Perhaps the name of the author—whose tragedy people haven't yet forgotten—will bring additional success."

She said with surprise, smiling, "You've really become a theater owner, Ezzat!"

Her remark annoyed him, and he said with some sharpness, "I've become a theater owner for your sake!"

"For *my* sake?"

"I mean for your sake and for his."

She gave him an apologetic look and said nothing.

The play achieved notable success, steadying the season after its initial stumble. The winter season passed without joy, but Ezzat succeeded singularly in the new season in Rod al-Farag—immoderate in his work as he was in all things—although without real happiness. Love continued to pursue him without the least hope. The opportunity presented itself, thanks to Farag Ya Musahhil, to rent the Elysée Theater on Dupré Street, and he rented it, moved by a spirit of adventure and obscure hope. He said to Badriya, "Here is an opportunity to work in the heart of the city. The time has come for you to shine like a true star."

20

He spent a lot of money preparing for the new season. The Elysée Theater was a good building in a good place. It had been shut for years because of differences among the heirs, until Khawaga Benjamin obtained it by a judicial decree, and Ezzat was the first to rent it in its new life. He felt as if he had become a theater owner in the true sense of the word, and that he would be working proudly in the domain of the Ramsis, Azbakiya, and Bintannia. True, he had not been able to bring any actor or actress of note into the troupe, but he had great confidence in Badriya. He continued to dream of a major success until opening night, when he suddenly received a cold shock as the curtain was raised to a house three quarters empty. At first he thought his troupe wasn't qualified to succeed downtown, but he heard that the theaters in general were suffering from slack and shrinking demand. All he could do was continue. Perhaps the single success ordained for the troupe came to Badriya, as a rich merchant proposed marriage to her! He heard that from Farag Ya Musahhil and not from Badriya, and that redoubled his chronic pain.

He met her alone in the manager's office, in an atmosphere heavy with disappointment, firmly intending to challenge her. He said, "Things are as you see. I wonder what we should do?"

She said sadly, "You shouldn't continue."

"Everyone is losing."

"All the more reason to take my advice."

"Should we go back to the Egyptian Club and Rod al-Farag?"

"If you like."

He said dubiously, "You aren't enthusiastic."

"Nothing calls for enthusiasm!"

He asked, with greater disbelief, "What about your future?"

She averted her eyes and did not speak, so he asked frankly, "Is it true what I hear about a man asking for your hand?"

She answered calmly, without raising her eyes, "Yes."

"Strange that the news should come to me from someone else!"

A movement betraying irritation escaped her but she did not speak. He said, "It's preposterous news."

"Why?"

"Didn't you say you were willing to wait a quarter of a century for the other?"

"Failure never crossed my mind."

"Is it true what's said about the man being thirty years older than you?"

"It happens."

"Maybe you are afraid of the effect of the recession, but we still have opportunities."

She stared at him openly and said, "The future is unclear, I want to keep my self-respect always, and then, I am alone. . . ."

He protested, "No. . . . No. . . . You are not alone."

They exchanged a long look, and he went on to say, "You are not alone, that statement hurts me."

"Thank you, but I am looking for a permanent, reasonable solution."

"There's a better solution."

"Really?"

"That we marry!"

She reflected a bit, and then asked, in a tone tinged with sarcasm, "Out of sympathy?"

He answered sharply and emphatically, "Out of love."

"Love?"

"The old love and the new love."

She said, staring at him angrily, "It's news to me!"

"If it weren't for all that's happened you would have seen it long ago."

"Was it there when Hamdoun was with us?"

His emotion shriveled and fell into ashes, and he didn't know what to say. After a period of suffocating silence he found a way out, and said, "The love returned once you were alone!"

Silence returned once more, freighted with suspicion and disbelief. He exhaled challengingly, and said, "It's stupid to make excuses for love!"

She asked him bitterly, "Who sent the letter to the prosecutor's office?"

His heart was ripped out in panic. He had not expected to be stripped of his clothes all at once. He realized what she meant, and he had forgotten nothing. But he asked, feigning ignorance, "What letter?"

"You know what I mean, it shows in your face."

"What do you mean?"

"You are the one who sent the letter."

"You're crazy."

"But it's true."

"It's delusion, and besides have you forgotten that he confessed before the letter arrived?"

She answered coldly, "But the letter was written and sent."

"A ridiculous interrogation with no basis."

She said calmly, "The marriage you suggest would mean continuing in crime, for you and for me also."

He said harshly, "The fact is that you don't love me!"

"That's also true. I have never in my life loved anyone but Hamdoun."

"But you won't marry that man."

"That's my affair. I have no other choice."

He said angrily, "I'll stop you."

She stood up, shrugging, and left, saying, "God be with you."

21

Badriya left. Work stopped. The lights went out. No longer was any voice heard, ringing with good or ill. The fantasy world collapsed, its magic evaporated. Sadness descended on every heart. He would not see her merry in her slave girl's costume. He would not be gladdened by a smile from her lips. Nor by the sweetness of her voice. A stony look of refusal was the last thing she had given him. An accusing farewell, stingy in tears. If she appeared it was the fantasy of one bereft. His breast had been sentenced to the torment of sterile longing. To savor the pain as a drunkard sips. To call on the unseen to turn away the mockeries of the unknown. Cursed be the day I saw you, cursed the day I returned to you. And the insidious, evil day I saw you in the kuttab. When wretchedness was ordained for me, the coddled lord. When the sparrows on the branches jumped in warning. Ain in her stupidity went about atoning for the stupidities of humanity. He had learned rebellion from the ancient fort, but with the heart of a naïve child. Lunatics and drunkards attested to your beauty, Badriya. And now the pressures of life do not permit the aggrieved to experience grief. He went to liquidate his work and dismiss his men with exceeding pain. Only Farag Ya Musahhil remained with him from his immediate past. Even Farag said to him, "The time has come for you to go back to your home and family."

How could he return with disappointment and crime and lost love? He said, "It's too late."

"Your place is there, and you'll find me at your service. You were created for distinction and honor."

"You want to send me back to idleness and affliction."

"Rather to distinction and marriage, and pilgrimage to the House of God!"

He answered, smiling, "I am now in the time of punishment; in a later life I'll act appropriately. Haven't you got any other idea?"

Quickly he went from one extreme to the other, asking him, "Have you got plenty of money?"

"Yes."

"Great, turn the theater into a nightclub, this is the time of clubs!"

"Do you have any experience with that, Ya Musahhil?"

"Some. The stage will stay as it is, the house will change, the concession will be enlarged. As for the girls and so on, leave that up to me."

He realized that he was plunging into dark depths. He was not afraid and he did not hesitate. He threw himself into the current of recklessness as if he were taking revenge on some unknown enemy. Ya Musahhil lost himself in deep thought, saying, "The profit is guaranteed."

He engrossed himself in changing the theater into a night-club. Builders and carpenters came. Agreements were made with girls and waiters and musicians. He fit the part of the administrator, with his growing stoutness and his acquired resolution. He moved from the apartment in Shubra Gardens to an apartment on Dupré Street itself. He provided himself with the food, drink, drugs, and women he desired. He was determined to forget Badriya as he had forgotten Ain previously, and likewise to forget his crime. He began to say to him-self that he had done nothing but guide justice to a killer.

Nonetheless, he was unable to dissipate a cloud of gloom or to silence a hidden voice of recrimination.

At distant intervals news of the neighborhood would come to him, exciting him and refreshing him. He would find in it something new, amid his nights crammed with pleasure, music, dance, and marvels. His mother was now advanced in years, but she had not lost her liveliness or her tireless charitable activity. She went about leaning on her umbrella or unfolding it, from lane to lane and from house to house. Popular imagination had granted her blessedness and saintliness, finally conceding to boundless admiration of her, for long life that defies time by its activity and capacities is worthy of admiration and esteem. She insisted on enduring, on youth. It was as if Sayyida had become the lady of the house, especially after the death of her mother. As for Samir, he made his way with a success suitable to atone for his father's fall; here he was now preparing to enter the school of engineering. Just as an immoral man can spring from the loins of a scholar, so can a scholar spring from the loins of the immoral.

Perhaps he wondered at times what had happened to Badriya. The passage of time had taken care of destroying his love, this time putting it to death, unlike the first time. He now realized that everything dies, and that what we really need is a bit of patience in misfortune. Perhaps today she was a mother concealed behind veils, or perhaps she was a widow, or perhaps she was divorced and homeless. What did it matter? She was nothing but a criminal. She was the killer of Yousif Radi. She was the one who pushed him to betrayal, she was the one who sent Hamdoun to his life sentence. What remained of her beauty? What was this thing called beauty that lived a few years? But it was ordained that man should suffer for no reason, and if it weren't for food, drink, and drugs, life on earth would be in vain.

Years passed. His profits mounted, his stoutness increased, eyes stared enviously at him, and he became serious in his flight from pain and depression. He believed that happiness was relief from inevitable pain, that man suffered pain for a reason and that if he did not find a reason he suffered naturally. And that hidden ennui trailed him, like the sound trailing after a carriage wheel, without a specific source. As for the happiest times, in fact they were the times of deep sleep. He stared suspiciously at laughing people, to the point that he imagined that his nightclub was no more than an abyss filled with the miserable and the mad. Would this life perhaps end in destruction and utter annihilation? He marveled at how he knew no one in his world to keep him company other than Farag Ya Musahhil.

Sleeplessness awoke him in the last hours of the night. His breast seethed with obscure, sad emotions. He suddenly decided to invite his son to visit him.

22

He waited in his elegant apartment on Friday morning. He did not imagine that he would fail to come. Even if the worst should happen, he would only be reaping what he had sown.

My dear Samir,

Do not be surprised. The writer of this letter is your father. You will ask, after all this time. But you do not know the depths of my life enough to have the right to judge me. Your father invites you to his home (3 Dupré Street, apartment 14) next

Friday morning (March 14). It is not right for us to have been separated this long time when we were in the same city. There are many reasons and you may have heard a lot but you don't know everything. I am your father in any case. We should get to know each other. It will give me great pleasure to meet you.

Ezzat Abdel Baqi

Neither Samir's mother nor his grandmother would prevent him from visiting. Ezzat put on his pajamas and robe, shaved carefully, trimmed his mustache, combed his hair, used his cologne, waited. At ten the doorbell rang. The ringing went to his heart, and he hurried to the door with his stout body. He opened it, and saw a young man whose identity he did not doubt for a moment. Ezzat's heart throbbed as never before. He opened his arms. At last the father and the son met and embraced. He went with him to the living room. They sat in armchairs facing each other, behind the closed door to the balcony. Between them was a table holding a generous platter with many sections, filled with fruit, nuts, and chocolate, a carafe of water, a bottle of Spatis soda, and a cup with a silver holder. They began to look at each other with interest and excitement, on the lips of each a radiant smile, quivering a bit in confusion. It pleased Ezzat to see him slender and inclining to height, and that he had inherited Ain's beautiful eyes, her long, high-bridged nose, and her high forehead. What a handsome young man he was, abounding in liveliness and intelligence.

Ezzat decided to end the silence, and said, "I'm very happy to see you."

Samir answered, in a voice that reminded him of Sayyida, "I'm happier, Father."

Laughingly, "No doubt you know things about me; perhaps they're unpleasant. I also know a lot about you. I have someone who supplies me with the news, so you can see that I haven't forgotten the family or the place. But let's set aside what disturbs our peace, let's protect our shared happiness as much as we can."

"That's the best thing to do."

"You're a student in engineering?"

"Yes."

"And successful in your studies, according to what I hear?"

"I have high hopes of being sent abroad to study."

He pointed to the table, inviting him to have something, and said, "Fabulous! Your father didn't like studying and wasn't successful with it. My entertainment was reading crime novels. But time always produces something better. Eat and drink, and tell me about your life."

He answered, pouring Spatis into the cup, "My studies are my main concern; during the weekends I play sports and read."

"Don't blame me for not asking about my mother or your mother, since I know everything about them. What do you read?"

"Various subjects—politics, literature, religion. I also like movies."

Laughing again, "And the theater?"

He pressed from his eyes the tears produced by the soda, ignoring the question, so Ezzat said, "That's why the theaters went broke. Are you interested in politics?"

"My whole generation is interested in it."

A serious look came into his eyes and he muttered, "Politics can cause tragedies!"

"Sometimes."

Ezzat said, reverting to cheerfulness, "I won't give you any advice, do you know why? Because I never took anyone's advice!"

Samir said, flooded with joy from the increasing familiarity, "How much I have longed to see you."

91

"Why didn't you satisfy your longings?"

"I thought that you weren't interested in seeing me!"

"A mistaken thought, one hundred percent, but you don't know everything."

He offered him an orange, then asked, "I didn't have many friends. And you?"

"I have a lot of them, in the neighborhood and in school."

"No doubt your relationship with your mother and grandmother is good?"

"As good as could be wished."

"Which is dearer to you?"

He smiled and said, "A mother is a mother, but my grandmother's charm is irresistible!"

"She's the eighth wonder of the world."

"How could you bring yourself to abandon her all this time?"

He said to himself that his son had not yet known distress or pain. Suddenly he took the plunge, asking him, "Why don't you tell me about your love life?"

Samir was confused and it looked as if he didn't understand, so his father took pity on him and asked, "It matters to me to know if you are happy."

"I think so."

"That's enough. I hope you are truly happy."

"I think so."

"Great, enjoy your time, because life does not stay the same."

The young man reflected for a while and then asked him, "And how are you, Father?"

"Successful, thank God."

"I mean, are you happy?"

Ezzat laughed aloud and said, "I think so!"

"I have a question but I'm afraid to ask it."

"Be as frank as you like with me."

"Are you married?"

"What do they say there?"

"They say you are married."

"And who is the wife they claim?"

"Badriya al-Manawishi!"

Ezzat laughed, hiding his emotion, and said, "Would I marry the wife of a friend in prison? Do you think your father would stoop so low?"

Samir answered in confusion, "Maybe it was decency and not lowness that . . ."

He cut him off, saying, "Your father has not married or thought of marrying."

Then, reverting to his smile, "What do you know about your father's work?"

"A nightclub owner."

"I wonder what they think of that."

Samir answered, laughing, "You know very well how people in our neighborhood are!"

"And I know your grandmother also."

"But she still loves you, you can't imagine how happy she was over your letter!"

"And you, Samir, give me your frank opinion about my work."

"It's honest work, Father."

"Maybe that's a textbook answer."

"But it's truthful."

"Doesn't it bother you for your friends to know about it?"

"They know!"

"You're a brave lad."

"Rather you are the brave one, Father."

"Really?"

"You do as you like without caring about people's opinions!"

They exchanged ambiguous smiles, and Ezzat wondered whether he might have preferred to find his father less stout and in cleaner work. He felt he was still in the first steps of acquaintance, and that the stiffness between them had not yet disappeared. He said, "After today you must not remain away from me a long time. I'll expect you every Friday."

Samir said, apologetically, "I promise you that, but beginning from the summer break."

Ezzat received his first disappointment, but he said, "Yes, exams are close, so be it. By the way, I've prepared a delicious lunch for you!"

23

With the entry of Samir into his life its structure was somewhat altered. In any case, it was not as it had been. The relationship between them grew stronger during the summer, turning into intimacy on a high level. He attained pure happiness on Fridays, and he was showered with sweet memories the rest of the week. He learned from him that he loved a student in the college of science named Ragaa and that he was going to announce his engagement immediately after finishing his studies. Ezzat was happy at the news. He welcomed the successful love and considered that he shared in it in some way. He congratulated his son on the good fortune he had been deprived of all his life. What might his life have been like if he had married Badriya when he wanted to? What clean, stable life escaped them both? Might not thoughts like these occur to her sometimes? As for what really troubled him, it was his son's interest in politics. Politics had become linked in his mind with treachery, crime, and loss. He said to him once, "Politics is very dangerous, Samir."

"Didn't you ever take an interest in it?"

"No."

"Do you think that's why you're so happy?"

He stole a glance at him because he thought he was mocking him, but he found him serious and guileless. He said evasively, "Politics took the only friend I had in the world."

"Hamdoun Agrama?"

"Yes. Have you heard of the group Tomorrow's Children?"

"Of course."

"It's a real tragedy."

Samir answered, smiling, "And a tragedy also that we don't take an interest in politics."

"He always said that. Isn't it enough for you to be an engineer and the head of a family?"

"There is no engineering and no family without politics!"

"Bravo . . . bravo. . . . There is something more important."

"Really?"

"It pleases me in my few moments of free time to wonder about the meaning of life."

"But politics gives you the answer!"

Ezzat laughed aloud and said, "It's hopeless, but excuse me, I have become a man of the past!"

"You are still young!"

Ezzat smiled bitterly. His son didn't know what he was saying. He didn't see this belly. Or these early wrinkles under his eyes, weakened by late nights, drinking, and drugs. He didn't know anything about the anonymous letter, or about the contempt the abandoned divorcée had for him, or her preference for an animal advanced in years. He resumed, asking, "What's the goal of politics?"

Samir answered after reflection, "It's the goal of every man: happiness."

"But there are easier and less dangerous ways to happiness."

"I don't think so. It's rare for a man to achieve self-realization and happiness like you!"

He answered with unexpected sharpness, "Please don't use me as an example!"

He remembered his mother in her everlasting persistence and her eternal rounds and said that the boy was the perfect image of his grandmother; they were both afflicted by a single madness, but each was unique. As for his life, it was a constant striving for a happiness that did not want to be realized. He had been given health, money, success, and women, and he lived pursued by a sly, hidden force. He said in a new tone, capitulating, "Do you know, son, it seems that the biggest mistake we make in life is to believe that the goal is happiness."

Samir asked him innocently, "What's the alternative?"

He said in perplexity, laughing, "I don't know."

"But you have experience with people and life."

"In the club I see only fools and madmen."

Samir laughed joyfully and Ezzat continued, "Perhaps the fault lies in that we are passing through a period of transition."

"Yes, our homeland. . . ."

But he cut him off, saying, "I mean man, he is capable of realizing his wretchedness."

"It's simple, all we have to do is remove the causes of misery!"

He raised his voice saying, "My friend Hamdoun lost his life doing that."

"Sacrifice . . . well, you must accept the value of sacrifice?"

He answered, laughing, "Certainly not, it's stupidity with no excuse but madness."

When he was alone with himself after Samir left, he said, "Oh, if only I could find the courage to admit my sin!"

24

Samir graduated as an engineer. He announced his engagement to Ragaa. He was selected as part of a group sent to study in England for two years. Ezzat invited his son and his fiancée to celebrate in his apartment. The atmosphere of the courtship penetrated to his depths—suddenly he longed for a stable married life. He found a new idea in his sudden longing, sly, but strong and captivating. But what bride would be suited to a man of his years? He loathed the women who visited his apartment from time to time. He wanted to lift the white veil from an innocent face in the prime of youth. Perhaps this was the last thing awaiting him in a series of mad adventures. The inspiration which precedes initiative descended on him. He remembered it, he had experience with it. Except that its springs ran dry when he bade Samir farewell. He kissed him and said, "It's not easy for me to be patient for two years."

His world was emptied of creatures and of life, just as it had been emptied the day Badriya disappeared. It was amazing that despite that he couldn't wait to realize his impulsive dream of marriage.

The narrator says:

Events gave him no respite, as was their custom with him always. When they came they hurled themselves upon him, as if wanting to finish their task in the shortest possible time. One morning his eye was attracted by this headline in the newspaper, "Arrest of a Cell of the Group Tomorrow's Children." For historic reasons, nothing more, a strong shudder went through his body and he was swept by a feeling of deep foreboding. He read the details with an interest and concentration at odds with his well-known lack of concern for that sort of news. This time he followed the news as if he were a member of this frightening group, as if the young people arrested were his associates, as if he had shared in editing, printing, and distributing the seized publications. The news of the arrest of the cell was presented as the first victory achieved by the security apparatus in this arena, and as the thread that would lead inevitably to the dens of the group wherever they were found. He went chasing the dark memories away from his sick imagination, cursing the weakness that afflicted his nerves. But he followed the news day after day until the official statement on the subject was issued. Many had been arrested, and there was serious pursuit of those who had fled.

Here was the statement referring to a new fact. No sooner did he read it than his heart fell into the abyss. In fact a loud scream escaped him in his empty apartment. There was talk about Samir Ezzat Abdel Baqi. Among the government-sponsored Egyptian engineering students in England. Who had fled England at the last moment for an unknown location. Ezzat began to pace hurriedly with his stout body, asking in amazement, Samir a member of the group Tomorrow's Children? Samir fled to an unknown location? Would Samir hide forever? Would he be swallowed up by wandering and homelessness abroad? Here you are taking vengeance on me, Hamdoun Agrama. I am experienced with these murderous games that take us unawares as we are progressing seriously on the way to happiness! Ezzat and Sayyida and Ain melting in a single crucible of wretchedness. What harsh, mad games they are, moved by a mocking devil. He was choked with tears, so he dried his eyes with a silk handkerchief, his initials embroidered on its corner. Farag Ya Musahhil consoled him, "In any case he had better luck than those who were arrested."

"I don't know. . . . I'm sure of one thing only, which is that I won't see him again in this life."

The man said with resignation, "Only God knows the unknown. Why don't you visit the lady?"

That had occurred to him as he was plunged in his sadness . . . to visit Ain and Sayyida. . . . But he quickly rejected the idea in anger and disgust. It wasn't the right time for playacting and acrobatics. Now he knew his destiny. To be divested of silly dreams of happiness, to beg for a vision that would not be realized, to carry out a life sentence of hard labor while residing among drunkards and pleasure seekers.

A new sort of fatigue crept over him, head and body alike. He suffered from a headache unknown to him previously. Perhaps the only benefit of that ferocious pain was that it forced him— even if only for a time—to forget his paternal crisis and to think about something else. For the first time he headed for a doctor's office. He discovered that he was suffering from very high blood pressure. Acting on the advice of the doctor, he agreed to enter the Islamic Cooperative Charitable Hospital to receive constant care until the danger passed. The goal of the treatment was to lower the pressure and reduce his weight by twenty kilos at least. Farag Ya Musahhil oversaw the club and visited him regularly. He would say, "Let me tell Sitt Ain."

This suggestion made him realize the danger and think about death. He imagined Ain sitting where Farag Ya Musahhil sat. Oh no, she would not leave the bed. A torrent of prayers, blessings, and Quranic verses would rain down upon him. She would say to him, "the time has come for you to change your life." She would say also, "I know the secret behind all this misery." Despite his impulsive yearning, worsened by lying in bed and thinking of death, he did not surrender. He said, "Do not tell anyone, not Ain and not anyone in the club."

"You think so?"

"Yes. . . . Carry this out precisely. . . . Not Ain nor any dancer nor any pimp!"

He began to receive warnings about obesity and food and drink; the forts in which he had protected himself from life and its eccentricities collapsed. They were stripping him of his weapons, and the illness was the ally of the punishments inflicted. It was strange that in his sleep he saw Sitt Ain's cats in the garden, and among them he saw Baraka with her haughty calm. He rejoiced and thought that he would surprise Ain with the happy news that Baraka was alive and had not died as she had imagined, and that she should not have cried. He woke that night at dawn with an unexpectedly heavy heart, like someone returning from a long, futile journey. It occurred to him that this world was a cat and that it ate its young, and he said aloud, in the peace of the night, "If Dupré Street and the Elysée are a prison then the neighborhood is no more than a cell!"

He left the hospital slender and lean, but sound. His underwear and clothes hung on him, and the world seemed to have changed color and grown cold, neither giving nor returning a greeting. He returned to thinking about Samir, but with complete resignation. He clung avidly to life despite everything, so he respected the diet, the medications, and his appointments with the doctor, and abandoned the bottle, though he did not give up the hashish pipe.

He had his clothes altered. He returned to his first slenderness, just as gray hair began to spread on his head, in his eyebrows, and his mustache. He looked mature and dignified, his dignity clashing with his environment and his work. Every time he remembered he had passed fifty he was astonished, disbelieving, and would summon unforgettable visions of the jasmine bower, or the kuttab of Sheikh al-Azizi, or of acting out the play *Romeo and Juliet* in the lane. He had thought that only happened to other people. It seemed that history was truthful in its assertions about the passing of peoples in ancient times and their disappearance. How long would we surrender to that and submit to it? But thanks be to long habit, for it had killed all sadness and all joy. Perhaps it was best for us to leave this world after we wearied of its boredom.

What of the neighborhood?

The informant continued to tell stories. Sayyida was still enfolded in the house, absorbed in her sorrows. Ain still persisted in her activity. But how absurd. She no longer went out more than once a week. Like a statue of eternal old age. When she walked she went in the company of a servant. What might still remain of memory, will, and intelligence? Which sorrow was harder for her, her sorrow over Ezzat or her sorrow over Samir? What did her deep-rooted faith make of these strange conditions? Had death ever found stronger resistance than it did at the hands of Ain?

25

The narrator says:

Ezzat Abdel Baqi did not expect anything new, unless it would be the curtain falling and the lights going out. But Farag Ya Musahhil visited him in his apartment one autumn morning and said to him, "I've heard strange news that might interest you more than anyone else."

Ezzat said, mockingly, "The club and everything in it is yours if you can arouse my interest!"

"It's news worth telling in any case."

"What is it?"

"Badriya al-Manawishi, the star of your old theater."

Out of what silence did that name emerge! The star of your old theater. There was no reaction. A star whose light reached him across long, long years, like the stars themselves, composed of a brilliant memory and an unknown present. What meaning did the news have? None at all, and no importance. He asked listlessly, "She died?"

Farag Ya Musahhil laughed and said, "Not at all, it's said that she was widowed two years ago or so and inherited a considerable sum of cash, but do you know how she invested it?"

"How?"

"Have you heard of the Nile Flower nightclub?"

"It's a club on a riverboat as far as I know."

"Badriya is its owner and manager!"

He smiled idiotically, stammering, "Amazing!"

"Maybe she was nostalgic for where she started out, or something like it."

"Or she was afraid of age and loneliness."

"Most likely she chose it to guarantee profit."

Ezzat laughed. Ezzat was the owner of the Elysée club and Badriya was owner of the Nile Flower club!

Moved by curiosity, moved by boredom, he decided to spend an evening in the Nile Flower. He said to himself, now I know why people want to visit relics of the past. He prepared with a warm bath, an elegant suit, a shave, and trimming his mustache and brushing his hair. He went to the Nile Flower. We are all the same age, Hamdoun and I and Badriya and Sayyida, and each has been allotted his fate fairly. Who is responsible for all our misery? I . . . or Hamdoun? Badriya? Sayyida? Shouldn't we be brought before a judge?

The riverboat had been turned into a club, extremely elegant and high priced. It attested to its founder's good taste and flair for imagination. He took his seat and his eyes began to explore the corners, the rows, and the stage; if his suspicions were correct, the manager's office was on the roof, reached by this spiral staircase covered with a red carpet. He asked for a bottle of champagne. He was the only one who was alone. Why had he come? Why not come? A young man sang in the Franco-Arab style; he was followed by a monologist, then a dancer. Would he spend his evening without Badriya appearing? He looked at the spiral staircase from time to time.

He became aware of the clicking of heels. The body began to appear slowly on the spiral staircase from bottom to top until it reached the head of the hall: Badriya al-Manawishi, who stood in attentive observation. A manager in the full sense of the word. He began to examine her. He was expecting a change, but not the change before his eyes. Fat as a headman's wife, her face so plump it aroused aversion. Gone was the freshness, the glow extinguished. At her age women retain remnants of beauty, but she retained nothing. Besides, what was the meaning of this look in her kohl-lined eyes? It was unnatural, was she sick? Her nerves unsteady, her memory gone? The result of a long, miserable history! Her eyes passed over him without stopping. It was best to ignore her and avoid her. But here she was tottering up the side aisle. In spite of himself, his eyes did not flee her. He had come and he had to take the responsibility. They were now separated by no more than a meter. Their eyes met. He was forced to smile. She stood astounded, not believing her eyes. It happened as fate had ordained. He moved his chair and stood. She whispered, "Good God."

He extended his hand and they shook hands. He indicated the empty chair, whispering in turn, "Please."

She sat down, stammering, "Al-Hussein help me!"

103

Ezzat laughed, asking, "Shall I order you a drink?"

"Certainly not. I've lost the habit. And you, haven't you had a drink yet?"

"No, and I won't, but because of illness."

"A speedy recovery. My health isn't all it should be either. But I didn't ever expect to see you. It seems that the living are fated to meet again."

His heart sank, remembering the wanted fugitive. He muttered, "Not always."

"What brought you to a club for young people?"

He answered heedlessly, "I came to see you!"

"How did you know?"

"There are lots of good people around."

"You were surprised of course, but there's more than one reason. What do you do?"

He answered, laughing, "I own the Elysée club."

She laughed aloud, not caring about the patrons!

He said, "Turning a theater into a club isn't a far stretch, but you?"

"Many reasons, among them the silly dream of presenting short plays and acting in them."

"Is it nice to have the yearning to act return to you after all this long time?"

"Just a silly dream."

"How was your life, I mean after we parted?"

She said shortly, "Extremely miserable, what with a hopeless husband and the hatred of his children and his family. And you, you're married of course?"

"No, just as you left me."

"You made a mistake, old man."

"Our lives are full of mistakes!"

"True. My entertainment is to watch the madmen who love the club."

"In the end they're annoying."

"But we can't live without them. How is your son?"

He answered, hiding his emotion, "Super . . . a top-notch engineer."

"Bravo. . . . That's the most important thing in the world."

"There isn't anything important in the world!"

Sighing, she said, "Do you remember the old days in the neighborhood?"

"Do you think they were happy, now?"

"Yes . . . and the successful days of the theater . . . my old love . . . my mother when she pickled limes, I wonder if the woman is still alive! By the way, what's the news of Sitt Ain?"

"She's well."

"Bravo! I wish I could visit her some day. Are you living in her house?"

"I haven't seen her since I left the neighborhood."

"No! However will we face our mothers on Judgment Day!"

He answered coldly, "Our paths were different."

"Of course, from artistic disappointment to nightclubs, we belong to the same type, and we got rid of the sound member at the right moment!"

He protested, "He's the one who got rid of us."

"He'll be released soon, if he hasn't been already. I wonder when he'll get out."

"I don't remember anything anymore."

"Don't you expect to see him?"

"I don't think so. Do you?"

"It doesn't matter. But what brought you here?"

"As I said, to see you."

"You still remember your old love?"

He smiled without answering.

She said sharply, "Love is a low-down lie, a rotten cheat. I think I only really ever loved the theater."

"Really? Even though it came to you by chance?"

"But I loved it, I never stopped loving it. In the miserable days of my marriage I would console myself by going off alone and repeating some of the roles."

"Creative consolation."

Laughing insolently, "You were a scoundrel and Hamdoun was a hero, and what was the result?"

He said, with a sharpness he couldn't contain, "And you were the devil behind us!"

"If the devil had married me success would have been our lot—he's better than the likes of you men."

He couldn't help but laugh, and that eased his tension.

She asked, "Why didn't you grow up like your noble mother?"

"My mother is one of a kind."

She laughed vulgarly for no reason, and said, "Your mother isn't the only woman like no one else. Listen well and judge for yourself."

She shook her dyed head gracefully and began to say, reciting in a low voice, with deliberation:

Friends, Romans, countrymen, lend me your ears.
I come to bury Caesar, not to praise him.

He smiled as if in a dream and muttered, "Beautiful!"

She swelled with his encouragement and continued, her voice a notch louder than before:

The evil that men do lives after them;
the good is oft interred with their bones.

The people sitting at the next table looked up at the voice, smiles appearing on their faces. Ezzat felt somewhat embarrassed, yet he whispered, as if enticing her to return to a whisper, "Everything will be interred with the bones."

She took no notice of his words, intoxicated with art, swept by memory like a wave of rebellion and recklessness. Her voice rang out in the wing of the club as she recited:

Come I to speak in Caesar's funeral.
He was my friend, faithful and just to me.
But Brutus says he was ambitious;
And Brutus is an honorable man.

Eyes stared at his table, necks craned from the other side. The true stage had moved to his corner. His forehead burned with confusion and shame. He pleaded, "Let's go to the manager's office!"

But she had gone beyond the time and the place. With her pitiable appearance she assumed a disdainful, challenging stance, and shouted in a voice that shook hearts and rafters:

But yesterday the word of Caesar might
Have stood against the world; now lies he there.
And none so poor to do him reverence.

The place rang with applause, applause of admiration, politeness, pity, and drunkenness. Ezzat begged her, "Enough."

She said, in dull-witted triumph, "All we have to do is return to the theater."

He said, wary of angering her, "I'll think about it."

"We have the money, Hamdoun will come back, what do we lack?"

"Great, great, great."

"Are you treating me like a child?"

"Never."

Sharply and resentfully, "Why did you come?"

"We should be friends."

"You are the worst memory in my life."

"God forgive you."

"Cowardly wretch."

"God forgive you, Badriya."

"Leave and don't come back!"

He complied with the order, rising and escaping with churning emotions. As for her, she went back to declaiming loudly:

Friends, Romans, countrymen, lend me your ears.
I come to bury Caesar, not to praise him.

26

He fled, wiping the sweat from his face with his handkerchief. What stupidity had driven him to the Nile Flower? Why hadn't he acted according to the wisdom that leads us to hide bodies in tombs? He had really not needed that painful experience, which had pierced him to the bone. Hadn't the experience of Samir, lost and vagabond, been enough for him? Alone in the manager's office he began to think about his life.

It was not the first time, but he was stirred to the point of inspiration. At first he had been depressed by leisure, but he had traded it for work he didn't believe in. Hadn't he? He was not a man of the theater, nor was he a nightclub man. "Work in my life represents flight from something or desire for something or vengeance for something," he mused. "My mother was the first one to lead me astray and she is pure good. I am not capable of understanding these things or digesting them. What I really need is peace of mind. What I really need is to be satisfied with myself. Does what they call satisfaction really exist? How can a man find it? Where will I find the answer to this question? What's the use of questions when I allow myself to be swept away in the current of daily life?"

It occurred to him to ask Farag Ya Musahhil as the two were smoking together in his apartment after hours. He asked, "Are you happy, Amm Farag?"

The man answered truthfully, "Thanks to God and thanks to you."

He realized that he had not understood what he meant, so he asked again, "What's the most important thing to attain happiness?"

"Health!"

"But that alone is not enough."

"Income."

"Nothing else?"

"A wife and children."

He had had enough of all of them and had fled them into the unknown. If he had wanted to remain and marry another he would have done so. No, it was more complicated than Farag Ya Musahhil imagined.

The telephone rang one morning in his apartment.

"Hello?"

"Ezzat Abdel Baqi?"

"Speaking. Who is this?"

"Don't you still remember Hamdoun Agrama?"

His heart throbbed with a mixture of troubled emotions, but he shouted, "Hamdoun!"

"Yes."

"I don't believe it. . . . What joy. . . . Congratulations . . . congratulations . . . congratulations. . . . Where are you now . . . ? Come right away. . . . I'm waiting for you."

A month or a bit more had passed since the Nile Flower experience. He sat waiting with a gloomy heart and an unwilling spirit, furious with the past that did not want to die. It seemed to him that he derived from his punishment a power that would change everything, and that he would refuse the humiliation of permanent captivity.

Hamdoun Agrama came.

He came as a different man, as he had expected, but beyond his expectations. He barely knew him. For the first time he saw him bald, his left eye narrower than the right, while his feeble gait and stiff right leg betrayed a paralysis that had once stricken him. His old sin stood before him, scowling and hateful, wresting away from him any compassion that might have been able to touch his heartstrings. He was swept by a hidden storm as the two embraced. That provoked him to think more about searching for a new life. He wanted to leave, and likewise he thirsted for the sight of Samir. He sat in the opposite armchair, in his son's favorite place. They exchanged glances, he smiling, the other still, or incapable of smiling with his slightly crooked mouth.

Ezzat said with delight, "God alone knows how happy I am to be reunited with you."

Hamdoun said in a low voice, "I expected that. I'm not well, but I'm happy to see that you're in good health."

Ezzat said, as if in protest, "No, I too have known illness. That's not what's important. Each of us has a story behind him and we'll have time to exchange them."

Hamdoun said, calmly and firmly, "But you are the father of a great son."

Ezzat was affected so deeply that he overcame his astonishment and inquired, "How do you know that?"

"Nothing is impossible for someone behind bars."

"What do you know about him?"

He said no more than before, "He's a great young man."

"I soon lost him."

He shook his head in denial and did not continue. Could Hamdoun know more about Samir than he himself did? He plunged ahead, perhaps without thinking, in order to shake his composure, "The latest news of Badriya is that she's working as a nightclub manager, the Nile Flower."

But Hamdoun was not affected. He asked indifferently, "How is she?"

"She's become old and senile!"

"A natural end, even if it has come a little early."

"Let's get back to you. . . . What are your plans for the future?"

"Not a thing!"

Even though he had expected that, he resented it. Nonetheless he said in a friendly tone, "Don't worry. . . . But you aren't well."

"Years ago I was stricken with partial paralysis, and I have no hope of any more improvement."

"How sad. . . . But there is hope. . . . You must be yearning to write!"

"I'm not capable of writing a single sentence."

"In any case, don't worry about making a living."

He said gratefully, "What a friend you are!"

Suddenly a change occurred like an explosion, unheralded and without any apparent cause. It took him out of time and place and threw him into hellfire, so he leapt up with a will of iron and shattered the barrier of lying. He shot up like a rocket, and said with a firm refusal, like a madman, "The letter was mine."

Amazement was written on Hamdoun's face. He asked, "What letter?"

"The letter of accusation sent to the investigator after you were arrested!"

A heavy, melancholy silence reigned. Hamdoun shot him a befuddled look and asked, "You?"

"Yes. . . . I know you confessed before it arrived but I'm the one who sent it."

Hamdoun swallowed hard and asked, "Why?"

"Ostensibly to serve justice but in fact to take possession of your wife!"

Hamdoun inquired darkly, "And you married Badriya?"

"No. We can never control a whole plan, since others share in making it, without our knowledge."

Silence reigned like a covering for diverse emotions, but Ezzat returned from his mad adventure with a certain calm and a great deal of acceptance, to the point that he asked, in the end, "What do you think of what you just heard?"

He answered scornfully, "You are dirty, but no dirtier than many."

He was not angry, accepting the rebuke as part of a refreshing stream of obscure intoxication. He stood on the edge of the challenge, his heart not without gaiety and inspiration. Expressing his new state he said in a voice that showed no displeasure, "We have an opportunity to forget the past!"

Hamdoun asked morosely, "Wasn't a quarter century enough to forget?"

"No."

"What do you mean?"

"That we deal with our affairs in a new spirit."

"Do you want to join our destinies again?"

"With sincere resolve."

He said scornfully, "You are looking for atonement and I despise that."

"Why did you come to me?"

"I never doubted you."

"We destroyed ourselves in the past, and now we must try to build."

He said, with greater scorn, "I must spit in your face."

Ezzat smiled, intoxicated by his capacity to endure. "I am responsible for you."

"You're incapable of taking responsibility for an insect."

"You should think again."

"I will not see you after today."

"How will you make your way?"

"Have you asked your son that question?"

Pain penetrated to the roots of his heart, so he refrained from speaking while Hamdoun continued, "Any tolerance on my part would mean that my life has gone to waste."

Ezzat said sadly, "I'm thinking about a new construction accommodating a healthy life that would include Hamdoun, Ezzat, Badriya, and Sayyida."

"You're trying to turn us into tools to create peace for yourself, just as before you turned us into tools of destruction, so that on our rubble you can erect a happiness that refused you."

Ezzat said passionately, "I've been repaid, with interest."

"If that were true you wouldn't think about us at all."

Hamdoun began to stand, leaning on his heavy cane with its rubber tip. Ezzat said beseechingly, "Give up your stubbornness."

He straightened his back leisurely. He moved to leave. Ezzat asked, "How will you make your way?"

He said, without stopping, "The way your son does."

His heart fluttered, and he asked apprehensively, "You know something about him. What do you know about my son?"

He answered, crossing the threshold, "Don't ask about what's none of your business!"

27

The narrator says:

Ezzat became another person. After Hamdoun left, the first Ezzat and the other one coexisted, living side by side in one place. They were completely identical to each other except that the First stared at the Other in amazement and perplexity, with a sensation of fear, and believing that the Other was also afraid of him.

He wondered how the current would carry them, when they were in one boat? For a period of a quarter century he had been accustomed to having his own opinion and this other acted like a partner, with enough confidence to challenge him. He heard him saying, "I won't go on."

He asked cautiously, "What do you mean?"

But the Other didn't answer him. He didn't seem to be concerned with his presence or to notice him. He said, as if he were speaking to himself, "I won't continue, that has become impossible."

He was plunging ahead with measures that had never occurred to the First. He said to Farag Ya Musahhil, "I'm leaving, you can manage the club if you like."

Farag Ya Musahhil stared at him, stunned, and the Other said, "I'm going to sell the furniture in my apartment and the art and so on."

The first Ezzat said to him, "You have no right to any of that."

But the Other acted like the sole proprietor. The First realized that he had no power to oppose him, so he advised Farag Ya Musahhil to obey him, to make him believe he was complying with his order and to keep everything as it was. At last the

Other embraced Farag Ya Musahhil in farewell, and Amm Farag said, "Going back to the neighborhood was what I suggested to you from the start."

The First was amazed, and asked him, "Are we really going to the neighborhood?"

The Other ignored him as usual and moved to the taxi. Before the taxi took off, the Other said to Farag, "My heart tells me that one day I'll be blessed with the sight of my son Samir."

The old man answered him, "You will find him as well as you might hope."

The taxi moved on its way to the neighborhood, the Other taking his seat inside it and the First following him closely. The taxi stopped at the entrance, so the two of them went into the neighborhood on foot. The First was amazed, and said to himself that hearing wasn't like seeing. How much the neighborhood had changed. The paving had been redone, with asphalt replacing stones. Lamps had been hung on the walls. The vacant lots had disappeared and in their place had been constructed homes and a school. It really did seem new, the girls striding by unveiled, in dresses. Only the tunnel and the old fort above it remained the same. Sitt Ain's apartment buildings had been newly painted. As for the door of her house, it sheltered slyly beneath the stuffed crocodile, its rough tanned hide giving no indication of the paradise extending behind it. No one noticed them, no one knew them. Two strangers in a strange neighborhood.

The First asked, "Wouldn't it have been better for us to travel abroad?"

But the Other knocked on the door. He entered with confidence, as if he were entering his house. An old servant recognized him, and shouted joyfully. The First said, "Soon you will see Ain. What have you got to say to her?"

The First was drawn—forgetting the Other—by the scent of the jasmine and henna. He saw a cat from the new generation, not Baraka or Nargis or Anaam or Abul Leil or Sabah.

"Here is Sayyida!"

She appeared in the passageway from which he had pulled her to the slaughter long ago. How much she looked like her mother today, in her old age, though she was thin and pale. Sad forever. I am the aggressor, not you. But it's you she's staring at, as if she doesn't see me. But you are staring at each other silently, under the pressure of memories. Then the Other said, "How are you, Sayyida?"

She was so agitated she did not answer. Her weak eyes were bathed in tears. Perhaps history had swept over her in a single moment, but at last she mumbled, "Please come to the balcony, the air is nicer there."

It was evening and the end of autumn, but the day was warm and he sat on the old sofa. Everything had changed except the house. There was the bower which had seen the childhood foolishness.

The Other asked, "Where is my mother?"

"In her room."

"Doesn't she know I have returned?"

He heard her breath rather than an answer, so he repeated the question. She said, "She does not leave her bed."

"Sick?"

"No, it's age."

"You should have taken me to her."

"You have to know a few things before that." He stared at her inquiringly, so she said, "She has lost her sight."

The Other frowned in distress, and the First realized how much had escaped Farag Ya Musahhil. Sayyida continued, "She has also lost her hearing!"

The Other stood, troubled, asking, "Didn't a doctor treat her in time?"

"Of course, that's the least one can do, but it's God's will."

The First said with grief, "Every homecoming has its price."

The Other plunged ahead to Ain's room. He saw her face above the green covering on the ancient, four-poster bed. The white kerchief had fallen away from silver locks. The face lay thin and long, embalmed by old age. He cried, "Mother!"

They both bent over her forehead and kissed it at the same time. A slight movement escaped her, and she whispered, "Sayyida?"

The First said to the Other, "A wasted trip."

The Other said sadly, "I'm Ezzat, Mother."

The First said, "You are only talking to yourself."

Sayyida said, "She never ceases to pray for you and Samir."

The First said, "Let's go abroad."

The Other returned to the balcony in the company of Sayyida as evening slowly fell. He said, "She will know me one way or another."

Sayyida said, "Slowly and gently, so that she does not become agitated."

She moved away a little so that she almost clung to the First without knowing it, and said, "I have to go."

The Other asked her, "Where to?"

"Any place."

He said resolutely, "But this is your home."

"But . . ."

He cut her off, "It's your home and it will be more so."

The First asked him, "Just what do you mean?"

As for Sayyida, she looked inquiringly at the Other, and he asked her, smiling, "Do you have any doubt that I've changed?"

She whispered, "Everything has changed!"

117

The First said to him, "Starting now you should write a long ode of lamentation."

Sayyida asked, "Isn't there any news of Samir?"

The Other said, "Nothing new. He's far away. My mother is also far away."

"If only I knew if he's alive and well!"

The Other said, under the influence of an inspiration coming from deep within, "He is, and we will meet again one day."

The First said, "We must go abroad."

For the first time Sayyida sat not far from the Other. They began looking at the garden together.

The First felt that the time had come for him to go, except that he heard Sayyida saying, "Sitt Ain has made a charitable trust of her property, to be set up when the time comes."

The Other reflected for a bit and then said, indifferently, "It was the best thing to do!"

"And she appointed you administrator of the trust, and after you, Samir."

He stammered, "Great."

She said, "When she was doing that, she said about you, He will practice charity willingly or not!"

The Other smiled and said, "I will do it willingly."

The First said to him, "I bid you adieu."

He left the house. He left the neighborhood. He went to Dupré Street. He rested a while in his apartment. He went to the club as the chanteuse was opening the evening, singing, "O rose and jasmine, by God O henna stem."

He threw a glance over the crowded room, then headed for the manager's office. No sooner was he alone than he said, "When Samir comes back he'll find three fathers waiting for him, I and the second and Hamdoun, and he will choose his father for himself, just as he's chosen his life."

He thought for a while and then said, "I will go abroad right after the end of the winter."

28

The narrator says:

On Lailat al-qadr, Sitt Ain was infused with unexpected energy. She refused to touch her supper of yogurt and asked Sayyida to sit her up. Sayyida folded a fresh pillow behind her back and placed her in a half-sitting position.

Ain said, smiling, "The air will be sweet and the earth will shine with the Lord's light, so care for the little birds with mercy." She continued smiling as she said, "I'm going to sing a song I loved when I was little."

She began to sing, in a weak, affecting voice, "Sweet dove, where will I get her?" Then she cried, "I can see. . . . I can see clearly."

The Other drew near and asked her anxiously, "Do you see me, Mother . . . ?"

But she continued without noticing him, "I can see the good ones who have passed. . . . They are calling me. . . . I hear and obey. . . . Ain is coming."

The narrator says:

Sitt Ain did not die. . . . Even though those who lived at the time of her death did not know her, or the majority of them didn't. They only know what the storytellers repeat. But Sitt Ain did not die. . . . and still today people call the hospital which arose on the site of her house 'Sitt Ain's hospital.'

Glossary

Abaya A long, loose outer garment

Abu, Umm Father, Mother [of]; used with the child's name in polite address

Amm Uncle; polite title for an older man

Aqsa Mosque The 'farther mosque,' the mosque in Jerusalem from which the Prophet Muhammad ascended to heaven on his night journey

Basbusa A semolina cake soaked in sweet syrup

Bastirma A form of cured meat

The Fatiha The first, short chapter of the Quran, recited in all formal prayers and to solemnize certain occasions, such as a promise of marriage between families

Fitiwwa (plural fitiwwat) A strongman who imposes his protection on a neighborhood

Fuul Broad beans, an inexpensive staple of the Egyptian diet

Gallabiya A long, loose garment like a dress, worn by both men and women

Al-Hussein The grandson of the Prophet Muhammad and third Shi'i imam; also an important mosque in Cairo, the plaza in front of it and the neighborhood around it

Iftar The first meal eaten at sundown after a day of fasting, in the month of Ramadan

Khamasin Strong seasonal winds in the spring, accompanied by duststorms

Khawaga A European or American, or someone who acts or dresses like one

Kuttab First school for children, where they are taught to read and memorize the Quran

Lailat al-qadr 'Night of the Decree,' between the 26th and 27th of Ramadan, when the Quran was first revealed to Muhammad; said to be a night better than a thousand nights, when prayers are answered

Mouloukhiya Jew's mallow, a green plant from which a favorite Egyptian soup is made

Al-Sayyida (Zaynab) Granddaughter of the Prophet, and a mosque in Cairo

Si, Sitt Titles of respect for a man or a woman

Spatis A brand of soda popular in Egypt in the 1950s and 1960s

Ustaz Title of someone with learning, especially western-style learning

Afterword

The events of Naguib Mahfouz's *In the Time of Love* take place in the early to middle part of the twentieth century in Cairo. During that period there was a thriving commercial theatrical movement in Cairo, both in the theaters downtown and in Rod al-Farag; the latter a district along the banks of the Nile north of the central city which was known then for its nightlife, especially during the summer. It is there that the careers of Egyptian comedians such as Naguib al-Rihani and Ali al-Kassar were launched, as well as that of the famous actress Fatima Roushdi, who was known as the 'Sarah Bernhardt of the East,' and who occasionally played men's roles.

The period is also known for a multitude of secret political societies, which Mahfouz depicts in various other works as well. Though the events narrated in this novel are fictitious, the historical context is nonetheless true to life.

I would like to thank Farouk Abdel Wahab, Nori Heikkinen, and Keith Miller for help with various aspects of the translation, as well as acknowledging the kindness of Neil Hewison, Nadia Naqib, and Noha Mohammed of the American University in Cairo Press.

Modern Arabic Literature
from the American University in Cairo Press

Bahaa Abdelmegid *Saint Theresa* and *Sleeping with Strangers*
Ibrahim Abdel Meguid *Birds of Amber* • *Distant Train*
No One Sleeps in Alexandria • *The Other Place*
Yahya Taher Abdullah *The Collar and the Bracelet*
The Mountain of Green Tea
Leila Abouzeid *The Last Chapter*
Hamdi Abu Golayyel *A Dog with No Tail* • *Thieves in Retirement*
Yusuf Abu Rayya *Wedding Night*
Ahmed Alaidy *Being Abbas el Abd*
Idris Ali *Dongola* • *Poor*
Radwa Ashour *Granada* • *Specters*
Ibrahim Aslan *The Heron* • *Nile Sparrows*
Alaa Al Aswany *Chicago* • *Friendly Fire* • *The Yacoubian Building*
Fadhil al-Azzawi *Cell Block Five* • *The Last of the Angels*
Ali Bader *Papa Sartre*
Liana Badr *The Eye of the Mirror*
Hala El Badry *A Certain Woman* • *Muntaha*
Salwa Bakr *The Golden Chariot* • *The Man from Bashmour*
The Wiles of Men
Halim Barakat *The Crane*
Hoda Barakat *Disciples of Passion* • *The Tiller of Waters*
Mourid Barghouti *I Saw Ramallah*
Mohamed Berrada *Like a Summer Never to Be Repeated*
Mohamed El-Bisatie *Clamor of the Lake* • *Drumbeat*
Houses Behind the Trees • *Hunger* • *Over the Bridge*
Mahmoud Darwish *The Butterfly's Burden*
Tarek Eltayeb *Cities without Palms*
Mansoura Ez Eldin *Maryam's Maze*
Ibrahim Farghali *The Smiles of the Saints*
Hamdy el-Gazzar *Black Magic*
Randa Ghazy *Dreaming of Palestine*
Gamal al-Ghitani *Pyramid Texts* • *The Zafarani Files* • *Zayni Barakat*
Tawfiq al-Hakim *The Essential Tawfiq al-Hakim*
Yahya Hakki *The Lamp of Umm Hashim*
Abdelilah Hamdouchi *The Final Bet*
Bensalem Himmich *The Polymath* • *The Theocrat*
Taha Hussein *The Days*
Sonallah Ibrahim *Cairo: From Edge to Edge* • *The Committee* • *Zaat*
Yusuf Idris *City of Love and Ashes* • *The Essential Yusuf Idris*
Denys Johnson-Davies *The AUC Press Book of Modern Arabic Literature*
In a Fertile Desert • *Under the Naked Sky*
Said al-Kafrawi *The Hill of Gypsies*
Sahar Khalifeh *The End of Spring*
The Image, the Icon, and the Covenant • *The Inheritance*

Edwar al-Kharrat *Rama and the Dragon* • *Stones of Bobello*
Betool Khedairi *Absent*
Mohammed Khudayyir *Basrayatha*
Ibrahim al-Koni *Anubis* • *Gold Dust* • *The Puppet* • *The Seven Veils of Seth*
Naguib Mahfouz *Adrift on the Nile* • *Akhenaten: Dweller in Truth*
Arabian Nights and Days • *Autumn Quail* • *Before the Throne* • *The Beggar*
The Beginning and the End • *Cairo Modern*
The Cairo Trilogy: Palace Walk, Palace of Desire, Sugar Street
Children of the Alley • *The Coffeehouse* • *The Day the Leader Was Killed*
The Dreams • *Dreams of Departure* • *Echoes of an Autobiography*
The Essential Naguib Mahfouz • *The Final Hour* • *The Harafish*
In the Time of Love • *The Journey of Ibn Fattouma* • *Karnak Café*
Khan al-Khalili • *Khufu's Wisdom* • *Life's Wisdom* • *Midaq Alley*
The Mirage • *Miramar* • *Mirrors* • *Morning and Evening Talk*
Naguib Mahfouz at Sidi Gaber • *Respected Sir* • *Rhadopis of Nubia*
The Search • *The Seventh Heaven* • *Thebes at War*
The Thief and the Dogs • *The Time and the Place*
Voices from the Other World • *Wedding Song*
Mohamed Makhzangi *Memories of a Meltdown*
Alia Mamdouh *The Loved Ones* • *Naphtalene*
Selim Matar *The Woman of the Flask*
Ibrahim al-Mazini *Ten Again*
Yousef Al-Mohaimeed *Munira's Bottle* • *Wolves of the Crescent Moon*
Ahlam Mosteghanemi *Chaos of the Senses* • *Memory in the Flesh*
Shakir Mustafa *Contemporary Iraqi Fiction: An Anthology*
Mohamed Mustagab *Tales from Dayrut*
Buthaina Al Nasiri *Final Night*
Ibrahim Nasrallah *Inside the Night*
Haggag Hassan Oddoul *Nights of Musk*
Mohamed Mansi Qandil *Moon over Samarqand*
Abd al-Hakim Qasim *Rites of Assent*
Somaya Ramadan *Leaves of Narcissus*
Mekkawi Said *Cairo Swan Song*
Ghada Samman *The Night of the First Billion*
Mahdi Issa al-Saqr *East Winds, West Winds*
Rafik Schami *The Calligrapher's Secret* • *Damascus Nights*
The Dark Side of Love
Habib Selmi *The Scents of Marie-Claire*
Khairy Shalaby *The Lodging House*
The Time-Travels of the Man Who Sold Pickles and Sweets
Miral al-Tahawy *Blue Aubergine* • *Gazelle Tracks* • *The Tent*
Bahaa Taher *As Doha Said* • *Love in Exile*
Fuad al-Takarli *The Long Way Back*
Zakaria Tamer *The Hedgehog*
M.M. Tawfik *Murder in the Tower of Happiness*
Mahmoud Al-Wardani *Heads Ripe for Plucking*
Amina Zaydan *Red Wine*
Latifa al-Zayyat *The Open Door*